"Hey, little lady...   ranger drawled in a husky southern accent that made Jessica think of molasses and gravel mixed together. *Mirages don't speak!* she thought in excitement, her heart leaping like a Norwegian salmon in spring. With his pomaded, fifties-style jet-black pouf, slanted gray-green eyes, and spiffy, royal blue silk shirt, the suave stranger was the answer to Jessica's prayers. And then some. A rescuer—and an ultra-swanky one to boot!

"I guess I do, mister," Jessica replied breathily, lowering her eyelashes demurely and almost unconsciously adding a cool, southern lilt to her voice. *Although I couldn't tell you where!* Not that it really mattered anymore. As the stranger got out of the car and Jessica's eyes flickered appreciatively over his long, lean physique and fitted-but-not-too-tight black dress pants, she already felt aeons away from Team One and all the bad memories she associated with the contest.

"Allow Elvis Presley to help you out, ma'am!" the stranger added, breaking into a grin that revealed flawless white teeth.

Bantam Books in the Sweet Valley University series.
Ask your bookseller for the books you have missed.

And don't miss these Sweet Valley
University Thriller Editions:

Visit the Official Sweet Valley Web Site on the Internet at:

http://www.sweetvalley.com

SWEET VALLEY UNIVERSITY®

Stranded

Written by
Laurie John

Created by
FRANCINE PASCAL

BANTAM BOOKS
NEW YORK • TORONTO • LONDON • SYDNEY • AUCKLAND

RL 8, age 14 and up

STRANDED

A Bantam Book / July 1999

Sweet Valley High® and Sweet Valley University®
are registered trademarks of Francine Pascal.
Conceived by Francine Pascal.

Produced by 17th Street Productions,
a division of Daniel Weiss Associates, Inc.
33 West 17th Street
New York, NY 10011.

ISBN: 0-553-49269-1

Published simultaneously in the United States and Canada

Bantam Books are published by Bantam Books, a division of Random
House, Inc. Its trademark, consisting of the words "Bantam Books" and
the portrayal of a rooster, is Registered in U.S. Patent and Trademark
Office and in other countries. Marca Registrada. Bantam Books, 1540
Broadway, New York, New York 10036.

PRINTED IN THE UNITED STATES OF AMERICA

OPM   0 9 8 7 6 5 4 3 2 1

To Ronald Pepple

Chapter One

"Come back, you morons!" Jessica Wakefield wailed, beating her fists in vain on the thick, bulletproof bar window as she watched Team One's Winnebago disappearing in a cloud of dust. A cold knot of panic twisted through her stomach as she ran over to the door and jiggled the lock one more time. No dice. She was locked in.

"Hey!" she yelled louder, rushing back to the window, but the Winnebago only shrank farther into the distance, barreling down the highway. Jessica blinked, disbelieving.

Are they completely stupid, or am I invisible? Maybe this is all just some kind of lame prank. And if it is, those jerks are going to get it—big time! Jessica vowed as she stalked up and down the empty bar. She wasn't exactly in the mood for jokes. It was bad enough waking up all alone in a beer-sticky plastic booth in a karaoke bar in the

1

middle of Nowheresville, South Dakota. Bad enough to discover that the Budweiser-for-brains bartender who was supposed to call her when her teammates returned had somehow allowed her to fall asleep and then forgotten all about her!

Or maybe he's in on the joke . . . ? Jessica hoped feebly, trying to reassure herself that things weren't as puke-worthy as they looked. Yeah, right! Another glance at the ant-sized speck zooming into the horizon confirmed her fears. No one was coming back for her. She was stuck.

What on earth was I thinking? Jessica smacked her open palm on the window. Looking back on it now—and literally looking at the back of the diminishing Winnebago—her decision to be part of Intense Cable Sports Network's summer Coast-to-Coast road trip contest seemed about as dumb as donating her summer to Greenpeace. *Not your finest hour!* Jessica chided herself, picturing a host of shopping sprees, Fourth of July parties, and potential hot guys she had given up. It was enough to make anyone want to drown themselves in drink. Especially if they were locked in a bar! But the very thought of a breakfast special of tequila shots was enough to make Jessica feel like hurling chunks. The bar reeked enough anyway, and all she wanted was a breath of fresh air.

As if on cue, a key jangled in the lock. *Saved by the moron!* Jessica thought venomously as the heavyset bartender lumbered through the door.

2

"Good. You've arrived," she snarled. "The service has been a little slow!"

"Uh—what are you doing here?" he mumbled, scratching his head in confusion.

"Oh, just enjoying the view." Jessica had to fight the urge to connect an ashtray with the guy's sloping forehead. "You locked me in, Einstein. Remember me?"

The bartender shuffled timidly toward the bar and started fiddling with a coffee machine. "Oh yeah. By the way, your friends didn't come back here last night. I think they must've hung out next door. They got a good jukebox next door. Sometimes people go there when they're sick of karaoke."

"Sick of karaoke?" Jessica repeated, her voice dripping with sarcasm. "Oh, that's impossible! Why, I just can't get enough of karaoke, as you can see!"

"Uh—coffee?"

"Listen, you big blockhead," Jessica snapped, her voice low and quivering with rage. "I got left behind because my teammates didn't realize I was here. So can it with the coffee and small talk and help me figure out what to do!"

"Funny your friends didn't notice you were missing," the bartender retorted, his voice calm and even. "They were parked right in front of the bar. Are you sure maybe they didn't get tired of your attitude and decide to leave you behind, missy?"

Jessica's eyes narrowed into slits. "You've got some nerve!" she shot back frostily. But inside her, a small seed of doubt began to harden and grow as memories of the night before—images she'd tried to keep down—pinpricked their way to the surface. Neil . . .

Jessica's face lit up like a halogen lamp at the very thought of Neil Martin. Everything had seemed so great between them. He'd made being stuck with a group of supremely uncool beings for four whole weeks totally worth the fuss and irritation. With his shaggy, coal black hair, shoulders that could span the Grand Canyon, and snappy sense of humor, Neil had seemed like the perfect sparring partner for Jessica. And it had seemed that he felt the same way. Jessica was convinced that anyone who'd seen her with Neil would have put out a major flirt alert on the vibe bouncing between them. Except for one little thing. Neil was gay.

Jessica still felt as if she'd been punched in the stomach when she remembered how much she'd fallen all over Neil the night before—only to be hit with a major brush-off. She could still picture the awkward look on his face when she'd confronted him with her feelings. He'd looked as if he'd rather be anywhere but with her, as if he wished the floor would turn to Jell-O and Jessica would sink right through it, her two-inch pink suede platforms leading the way to the underworld. . . .

He probably wishes we'd never even met! Jessica thought miserably, cursing herself for letting her heart lead her into such an embarrassing mess. The only thing worse than complete and total rejection was complete and total humiliation. And maybe Neil felt it too. Maybe he was mad at her for forcing him into revealing such a personal part of himself. And maybe he'd decided the entire team would be better off without her.

But how could I have known? Jessica wondered, swallowing hard to keep from breaking down into a sniveling wreck. It wasn't like Neil hadn't responded to her signals. He'd seemed just like any other guy Jessica had ever been interested in—interested in her. There was no warning sign in his behavior, nothing but the usual adoration Jessica was accustomed to getting from the guys she liked. Or maybe the famous Jessica Wakefield intuition was short circuiting! Jessica's eyes widened in fear. If that was true, she was as good as nailed into her coffin. Jessica minus her guy-dar was like a shoe without a heel—in other words, useless!

The thought was so terrifying, Jessica had to banish it from her mind. *Get it together, Wakefield,* she ordered herself, dismissing the tears of self-pity welling up behind her eyelids. *You're not helpless!* she told herself sternly. OK, so maybe she'd just lost her pride and a good friend all in one lousy evening. And maybe she was in the middle of nowhere. And maybe her team had purposely ditched her, left her behind. *Whatever! You don't need them!* she told herself. *You've got a driver's license and a credit card. You can rent your own wheels and pull a proactive Wakefield maneuver on them all!*

Jessica brightened at the thought of spinning down the highway in a convertible. It would be fun—and she'd get free highlights from the beating rays of the sun as an added bonus. Thank goodness for American Express! Jessica sighed with relief as she raced over to the booth in search of her purse. But her purse was nowhere to be seen.

Jessica gulped as another unwanted memory prodded at her. Her purse was in the Winnebago!

"This is just great!" Jessica moaned, recalling how she'd slung her stuff into the Winnebago before going back into the bar. And far worse, she calculated, she had no clothes with her either. A major fashion and financial disaster! The same outfit two days in a row. Maybe even a week. Jessica felt as if Stephen King himself had personally designed this horror story for her. *Cash flow is one thing, but pink capri pants for the rest of my natural life?* she thought in dismay. *This is purgatory!*

Defeated, Jessica lay down in the booth, helplessness descending on her like a bad hangover. *If only Liz were here* . . . Elizabeth would know what to do. And she'd be dead calm too. Although the twins were identical, from their thick, honey blond

6

hair to their blue-green eyes, Jessica had to acknowledge that Elizabeth was way more levelheaded than she. In the past the practical side of Elizabeth had always gotten on Jessica's nerves. But right now Jessica would give up all of the qualities that made her an exciting woman of the world for just one ounce of Elizabeth's practicality.

Or maybe I don't have to! Jessica realized in excitement, sitting up and looking out the dirty window. Through all the drama of being left behind, Jessica had totally blanked on the fact that Team One wasn't the only team driving to the next event stop. Whatever dreary, midwestern one-horse town was next, everyone had to get there, including Team Two.

But just as suddenly as Jessica had thought of it, all hopes of being rescued by Elizabeth dissolved. She didn't see a single other RV parked outside. Team Two must have left before Team One—and so had everyone else. *Liz could be eating Eskimo Pie in Alaska by now, for all I know!* Jessica thought bleakly, nervously peeling the frosted baby blue nail polish from her thumb. One thing was for sure, wherever Elizabeth was, she was miles away from Wonderlust and totally unaware of Jessica's plight. *I'm nothing but a distant memory,* Jessica thought, letting out a loud wail of despair. It was all too much. She might as well close her eyes and die.

"OK, missy, put a muffler on those lungs and

tell me where you're headed. Maybe I can give you a ride." The bartender held out a mug of stale-smelling coffee, but Jessica turned away from him. *Great! Now the crown prince of Dorkdom thinks he can rescue me!* she thought.

"Look, I'm going miles away from here, buddy. And I doubt you've ever even left your hometown," Jessica added airily, still hopping mad that the guy had managed to lock her into the bar and then act so cool about it and not even apologize!

"So where are you going, big-city girl?" the bartender replied, chuckling.

"Far away from this place, that's for sure," Jessica snapped. "Although the next stop is proba- bly even worse," she muttered glumly, watching as the bartender began to sweep the floor. "All I know is that it's some hole-in-the-wall, poky little town with the extremely appropriate name of Wall."

"Huh?" The bartender stopped sweeping and shook his head. He looked seriously confused. *Slower than a two-toed tree sloth,* Jessica thought disgustedly. *And I'm supposed to believe he can help me get to the next stop in time?* But what choice did she have? The whole scene was a level nine point nine on her personal tolerance scale.

"OK, let me just ask. Do you have rubber for brains?" Jessica retorted caustically, holding up a hand in irritation. "Because I'm, like, bouncing things at you and they're just coming right back!

Allow me to repeat," she continued with exaggerated slowness. "Wall. Would you like me to spell it? Those one-syllable words can be tricky."

The bartender couldn't resist a little smirk. "Hey, hold the sarcasm, honey. You're the one who's confused. You've already been to Wall. That's where you ICSN people did the event at the drugstore. This is Wonderlust, just outside of Wall."

"Oh yeah? Well, Wall, Wonderlust—obviously they're instantly forgettable!" Jessica tossed her hair and tried to act nonchalant, but inside she was triply cringing. *Why am I being so spacey?* she wondered, irritated to have been shown up in front of the bartender. *Obviously the negative IQ around here is catching,* she thought desperately. *All the more reason to lose this joint!*

"So, are you going to tell me where you need to go," the bartender continued, "or do we citizens of Wonderlust have the pleasure of your company for good?"

Jessica opened her mouth to reply but found herself suddenly at a loss for words. Her mind was a total blank. *Think, Jessica,* she coached her brain. *They announced it yesterday!* But no matter how hard she tried to remember the next Coast-to-Coast event stop, doing her best to recall the TV voice of Richie Valentine, Intense's live anchor and most popular on-air personality, all she got was a headache.

You've got to remember! Jessica tried to focus,

9

but a sickening feeling came over her, and she felt her throat begin to constrict in panic. It was no use. She had no idea where the next event stop was. She ran a shaky hand through her hair and looked miserably at the bartender. No money, no clothes, and not the faintest clue where to go. *Now I've lost everything!* she thought, her bottom lip beginning to tremble. *First Neil, then the team. What's next?*

"Can I help you with something else?" the cashier asked with an impersonal glance.

How about guy trouble? Elizabeth thought ruefully, but she merely shook her head and grabbed her coffee. Pretty embarrassing to zone out in front of anybody and everybody at the rest stop, but she'd been acting weird all morning. No matter what she did, her brain wouldn't switch onto normal.

Throughout the morning's drive from Wonderlust, South Dakota, to North Platte, Nebraska, Elizabeth had fixated on the same issues running around and around in her head on an endless loop. She felt like a hamster on a wheel. And she had Sam Burgess, Mr. Mixed Message himself, to blame for it.

What was Sam's problem? Why did he breathe hot one moment and cold the next? What was all this she'd just heard about a girlfriend in Florida? If he had someone else, then why had he kissed

Elizabeth the night before? Why had he pulled her into his arms so forcefully, drawn her close to him, kissed her so passionately? *And why do I care?* More than anything, this last question seared into Elizabeth's heart like a branding iron. It was so unlike her to be intrigued by such a complicated guy, the kind of guy who spun your head around. The type who enjoyed the conquering more than the conquest. Elizabeth winced. *Jessica's type— maybe—but certainly not mine!*

Elizabeth sugared her coffee and shook her head in defeat. She barely recognized herself anymore—drawn to an arrogant guy who obviously didn't know what or who he wanted. *But he's got another side,* Elizabeth found herself thinking, remembering how honest and sincere Sam had been only days ago, crying on her shoulder, admitting he'd been so harsh about the white-water rafting incident only because he'd been so worried about Elizabeth's safety. He'd seemed like a whole other person in those moments—intense and together and honest—someone Elizabeth could really relate to. *Maybe he* was *a whole other person!* her inner voice retorted. *And maybe that other sensitive Sam is all a big act!*

Elizabeth bit her lip, waiting for the inevitable gearshift in her thoughts. It was true, Sam could seem to be nothing more than a callous manipulator. But perhaps being aloof was just his way of masking his own vulnerability—a silly, macho

11

front to protect himself from having to open up to anyone. Elizabeth sighed deeply and took a long sip of her coffee. This kind of circular reasoning led nowhere, she knew. She couldn't be a fair judge of Sam's character. His behavior was way too paradoxical to figure out.

Like now. Sam was doing an excellent job of avoiding Elizabeth, even though they were on the same team and had traveled in the same Winnebago all morning.

He still won't meet my eye! Elizabeth observed as she spotted Sam sitting at a corner table, looking out the window. He was trying to pretend he hadn't seen her, but she knew he had. There weren't exactly hundreds of people in the rest stop—just Josh Margolin and Uli Lundstrom from their team and a couple of truckers milling around.

Despite herself, Elizabeth almost giggled as she watched Sam, intent on looking out into the parking lot, as if it were the most incredible view. Drop the act! she felt like saying to him. After all, how long could he avoid someone who was living with him in the same cramped Winnebago?

Not for much longer if I can help it! Elizabeth boldly walked toward Sam, trying to look determined but relaxed. There was no sense in getting herself into a knot of guessing games. Sam was the kind of guy who clammed up if you pushed too hard. But maybe if she just sat down and asked him what was up, he would see that she wasn't trying to cramp his style. *I just want the facts!* she told herself. Years of reporting for both Sweet Valley High's and Sweet Valley University's newspaper had taught her that every side deserved to tell its own story. And Elizabeth was nothing if not fair. Sam was about to get his chance.

Here goes, she thought. But just as Elizabeth felt a surge of cool confidence, Sam turned his head to meet her look head-on, his hazel eyes resting on her for just the briefest moment before flicking away to stare at the wall behind her. A brief moment, but it was long enough for Elizabeth's heart to suddenly kick into an arrhythmic beat. What was it about him? She couldn't put her finger on it. Maybe it was the unaffected but piercing intelligence that Sam seemed to barely even know he had. Or maybe it was just the way his sandy hair kept falling into his eyes when he got absorbed in his own thoughts . . . Whatever it was, Elizabeth felt as if she'd been thrown into a tumble dryer every time he looked at her.

But don't let him throw you, she cautioned herself as she neared his table. If Sam saw how nervous he made her, Elizabeth knew she'd get nowhere. He'd just cut her down to nothing with a few well-chosen words—if she let him! Elizabeth lifted her chin and strode purposefully in Sam's direction. She felt strong, and she hoped it showed. Either way, he wasn't going to get the better of her. . . .

"Hey, Liz, what's up?" A booming voice

13

interrupted Elizabeth's motivational moment as Josh cut across her path and flung an arm around her shoulders. Elizabeth tried not to look too irritated, but the truth was, Josh managed to yank her chain without even trying. Perhaps it was his slightly too slick appearance or the way he always seemed to bring out the jocky, bragging side of Sam. Elizabeth also resented the way Josh insinuated himself into every situation even when he clearly wasn't needed or wanted.

"Man, do I feel pumped for St. Joseph!" Josh babbled, pushing his mirrored sunglasses up onto his dark, oiled hair. "I hope they've planned something big because I'm up for a mean challenge, and I'm feeling red-hot. We can't afford to slack off just because we won in Wall, you know," he added. "Team Two's still only third overall!"

"Uh-huh," Elizabeth replied tonelessly, taking a giant swig of her cooling coffee. She was hardly in the mood to discuss the competition with Josh, and right now she wasn't able to muster any enthusiasm for trying to guess the next event. Frankly, she couldn't care less what tricks the committee had up their sleeve or how far behind Team Two had fallen.

"Whoa, go easy on the caffeine, Liz," Josh continued jokingly. "Although on second thought . . . you do look beat. Worn out from last night?" he added with what seemed to Elizabeth a conspiratorial wink.

14

Elizabeth felt her cheeks flush to a burning shade of crimson, and she quickly looked away from Josh's playful but penetrating gaze. *Everyone knows!* She should have realized that everyone in the karaoke lounge must have seen Sam send Todd away. Seen Sam pull Elizabeth to him on the dance floor, kiss her with an almost brutal passion. Seen Elizabeth return his kisses with an equal passion. So of course Josh would be joking at Elizabeth's expense.

"Hey, take a seat, sleepyhead!" Josh gestured toward Sam's table, but Elizabeth shook her head and set her coffee cup on a different table.

"I'm fine here," she added coolly, sitting down and trying to ignore the flashback from last night that was worming its way to the forefront of her thoughts. Sam's kiss had been so forceful—but also in its own way surprisingly gentle, as if he was making up for all the insults he'd given her that should have been kisses. And as his lips had touched hers and his fingers had wound tightly through her hair, Elizabeth's stomach had dropped and fallen away as if she were on a roller-coaster ride.

Obviously the kiss meant nothing to Sam, Elizabeth thought numbly, staring at the peeling tabletop. *Maybe I'm just passing entertainment until he can be with the real thing!* Elizabeth berated herself silently for allowing her emotions to overcome her. If there was one thing she wasn't

15

used to feeling, it was jealousy. And especially not for some girl named Angelina in Florida whom she'd never even met. Whom she'd only over-heard Sam and Josh talking about. But it was hard not to feel out of control and insecure when Sam held all the cards and she had nothing but a bruised ego.

So confront him! Elizabeth's inner voice insisted for the second time. *Don't be so passive!* Nervously Elizabeth plucked at a stray thread of her turquoise, cotton-knit sweater. She was still torn between wanting to deal with Sam and wanting to hightail it out of there. But the one thing she did know was that leaving things hanging would only wind her up tighter until finally she snapped.

Elizabeth stood, and even though her feet felt like blocks of lead, she forced herself to walk toward Sam. She was going to get some answers, and she wouldn't let him or his friends intimidate or embar-rass her. She was simply going to walk up to Sam, ask Josh to let them speak in private, and then level with him. No histrionics, no emotional venting. Just a straight-up, yes-or-no cross-questioning session with Elizabeth in charge.

But as she neared the table, Elizabeth's confi-dence began to falter. Josh and Sam were laughing loudly, unfazed by her approach. *Or maybe they're laughing at me!* Elizabeth chided herself for being hypersensitive, but her hands began to tremble. And then Sam turned to look at her, and although

16

his expression seemed blankly impersonal, Elizabeth thought she could detect the hint of an ironic, belligerent smile at the corners of his full lips.

That was all she needed. Her hands began to shake even more violently, and to her horror, she felt the plastic-foam cup slip from her grasp and fall to the floor. Elizabeth dropped to her feet and reached for the cup, tears of pain and humiliation stinging her eyelids as the brown liquid seeped through her clothes. She'd made a fool of herself in public. And all because of Sam. So much for being in control!

Once again, Sam had won.

"Oh, Robbie-pie," cooed Pam Cox. "We're in Valentine! Isn't that just soooo romantic?"

Not when you say it! Neil thought sleepily, burying his head in his pillow to try to escape the sound of Pam's shrill, squeaky voice. Deciding which part of Pam was the most irritating was a tough call, but Neil figured if it came down to it, her Fran-Drescher-on-helium vocals would definitely take the prize.

At least he was awake now, although a fire alarm would have been much friendlier. Neil stretched and sat up in his bed. Squinting blearily out the window, he saw Pam Cox and her boyfriend, Rob Baxter, giggling and cuddling at the side of the road. *The ubiquitous Kodak moment,* Neil thought in amusement, pulling on a pair of sweatpants. *Bizarre species captured in road-side embrace!* Pam and Rob were notorious for having big, messy, drawn-out tiffs, and when Neil last checked, they were in the middle of yet another breakup—a now all-too-familiar epic saga of classical Greek proportions. But they always made up—an equally theatrical rerun involving much exaggerated, starry-eyed behavior on display.

"I see you lovebirds are feeling chirpy this morning!" Neil called as he stepped out of the Winnebago and joined Pam and Rob by the side of the road. "Where the heck are we?" he continued, stifling a yawn. "I feel like I'm still asleep."

"Valentine, Nebraska!" Pam squeaked, pointing a nail-bitten index finger at the road sign above them. "We've passed the state border. Good-bye, South Dakota, look out, Missouri!" she squealed, flipping her mane of frizzy orange hair and jumping into Rob's outstretched arms.

"Pretty impressive," Neil remarked. "That we've crossed the border, I mean," he added, wincing as Pam and Rob practically devoured each other in a major clinch. Not exactly the view he'd been hoping for first thing in the morning. He turned away from the groping couple and headed back into the Winnebago, almost bumping into Todd Wilkins as he made for the camper's tiny kitchen.

"Nice job on the driving, Todd," Neil said, pouring half a bag of coffee grains into a filter. "I

18

hadn't realized we'd gotten so far. I was out like a light."

"Well, someone had to get this show on the road," Todd grumbled, grabbing a backpack from under a seat. "And considering I feel like my head got squeezed in the juicer, I'm as amazed as you are that we made it this far."

Somebody's tense! Neil observed, noting Todd's scowl as he rummaged around in a toiletry bag, obviously frustrated by not finding whatever it was he was looking for.

"Great!" Todd muttered. "The hangover from hell, hours of driving while the rest of you got your beauty sleep, and now someone's flattened the Tylenol. This trip is turning out to be a major waste of energy!"

"Sorry, buddy. Can't help you there. Maybe Pam or Rob has extra," Neil volunteered in a soothing tone of voice. Best to tread lightly. Todd wasn't exactly having a sunshiny day.

"Nope. Already tried everyone except Jessica," Todd answered irritably. "Unfortunately Princess Wakefield is still dead to the world. Maybe someone put a pea under her royal mattress and she had a bad night."

A bad night about qualifies it, Neil thought grimly. Under normal circumstances Neil might have found Todd's quip amusing, but not this morning. Just being reminded of Jessica—whom his groggy, morning-clogged thoughts had managed to overlook—was enough to jog Neil's insides, snap open his eyes, and bring him up to speed faster than a triple hit of extra-strong espresso roast. And the memory was far from welcome.

Neil knew he should have told her sooner. But he could never find the right time or the right way to let her know he was gay. It wasn't the sort of thing you just blurted out to a new friend. And even though he'd suspected she had some kind of a crush on him, he hadn't been sure about it until they were at the karaoke bar last night, where she'd clung to him like metal filings to a magnet and announced her true feelings. There had been no ducking it then. *But you could have been more sensitive.* Neil sighed guiltily as he recalled the hurt look on Jessica's face and then the way she'd turned scarlet with mortification. *So much for tact and social sophistication,* he chided himself. *If Intense Coast-to-Coast were giving points for bluntness, you'd take your team to victory!*

Unfortunately, Neil didn't know how else he could have finessed the situation. He'd wanted to tell Jessica his secret for some time. They had a real rapport, and Neil knew he could trust Jessica with information that intimate. But at the same time Neil knew that in telling Jessica, he risked losing their friendship.

Were we too close? Neil wondered. It was possible. But if he had led Jessica on, he hadn't done it intentionally. It was just the result of grooving well with someone, someone who could appreciate his aesthetic, someone who took life with a boulder of salt like he did, someone who generally handled life's daily ups and downs with the same ease. *And if there's anyone I can relate to, it's Jess!* he reminded himself. Jessica was a tough girl with a straight-up attitude and an inimitable wisecracking flair for handling every social situation. It had been obvious from the word go that they were going to click. *All the more reason to have come clean sooner,* he chided silently. *But you were gutless!* Neil couldn't help being angry at himself. But he still felt raw whenever he even considered coming out. You never knew how the people closest to you would react— which was why he hadn't told anyone on the team yet. And maybe never would. Judging by Jessica's reaction, he realized that telling the truth could mean the mother of all train crashes. . . .

"When is the delicate rosebud going to surface?" Todd queried resentfully, breaking into Neil's thoughts. "Wakefield's my only hope for deflating the expanding balloon that used to be my head."

"Jess is definitely a walking medicine cabinet," Neil agreed, forcing a smile to his face. *Keep it light now. Deal later!* he told himself, throwing on a faded Stanford sweatshirt.

"Yeah, but the catch is, she's also a walking headache," Todd retorted irritably. "So I'm screwed either way!"

21

"Looks like it, buddy, but chill out, would you? You're not the only one with a hummer," Tom Watts interjected as he entered the kitchen from the front of the Winnebago. "And I've been squinting at maps all morning," he continued. "So cool it on the martyr front."

"Hey, it's your fault I got so wasted anyway!" Todd shot back, folding his arms huffily, his bloodshot brown eyes narrowing to slits.

Two testy copilots driving this ship! Neil noted, standing back as the guys glared at each other. Tom and Todd had actually seemed to get along for the first time ever the night before, but now it looked as if they'd taken fifty steps backward. And someone had to defuse things before they got out of hand. After all, there were still three weeks left in the competition—three weeks of everyone living in each other's pockets.

"Whoa, guys, Zen down a little," Neil broke in cheerily, pouring two mugs of steaming black coffee and handing them to Todd and Tom. "You're both gonna be fine. And it could have been worse. You could've been talking to the great white telephone."

"Huh?" the two mumbled in unison.

"Euphemism for hurling into the john—at least where I go to school!" Neil replied with a grin. "And now if you'll excuse me, I'm going to head over to that goose-down lump otherwise known as Wakefield and see if I can get her to join the land of the living."

22

Although his heart felt as if it was ready to jump out of his rib cage and do the funky chicken, Neil took a deep breath and headed through the dividing door that separated the bunks from the kitchen area. *Maybe after a good night's sleep and a good strong cup of java, Jessica will see that all is not lost!*

"Hey, time to come out of that coma," Neil joked in a gentle voice, sitting on the edge of Jessica's bunk. But Jessica didn't so much as stir. *She's probably just faking, hoping I'll go away,* Neil thought. But he was determined. They had to hash it out sooner or later, and in his opinion, sooner was always better than later. "Look, Jess, I know you're not exactly dying to clap eyes on me right now, but please don't shut me out." Nothing. "At least drink the coffee I made you," Neil continued teasingly. Still not a rustle.

"Jess! You can't avoid me forever, you know," Neil said, his voice rising with emotion. "We've got to talk this thing out. And I can't talk to you if I can't even see you!" He touched the top of the comforter and peeled it back slightly. But instead of the partially exposed silky blond head he expected, he found only a fluffy white pillow. *Huh?* Neil's face twisted in confusion. And then it hit him with a dull, sickening tingle—as if he'd banged the funny bone in his elbow.

Jessica wasn't in her bed, and she wasn't in the Winnebago. She wasn't anywhere nearby— because she was still in Wonderlust.

23

But how? Before he had time to further contemplate the question, Neil heard raised voices. Tom and Todd arguing over where the next rest stop should be.

"OK, Pam, Rob, time to cut the bonding and get in the Winnebago," Todd yelled. "Everyone, we're moving on!"

Numbly Neil walked out to face the group. "Not so fast," he began weakly, swallowing hard as everyone looked at him expectantly. "Guys, we have a problem." He closed his eyes as if he could wish the whole twisted chain of events away. A day ago everything was peachy, and now it had all gotten pear shaped. And he was responsible!

"What, did our resident Theta queen break a nail?" Pam retorted sourly.

Neil felt beads of perspiration forming on his forehead as he struggled to keep his cool. "No, Pam. There's a slightly bigger problem," he replied darkly. And that had to be the understatement of the millennium.

Now I know why they call it the Badlands! Jessica reflected huffily as she stomped down the highway. Because it was very, very bad! A shocking excuse for a landscape!

If that was even where she was. Jessica didn't know, and she didn't exactly care. At least she was out of Helltown, USA. Not that she'd gotten very far. Jessica squinted in the baking sun and regarded

24

her surroundings with distaste. Nothing but flat, scrubby landscape and miles and miles of emptiness, broken only by the occasional black rock.

Why did we even bother to colonize this place? Jessica fumed, sweat trickling down the back of her white, stretch-terry halter neck. *Those explorers obviously didn't have a brain cell among them. They should have taken California, Florida, and New York and left out the rest!*

And apparently the rest of America agreed with her because not a car had crested the horizon since she'd started her great trek. A whole hour with only scuffed pink suede heels and streaky mascara to show for it. So much for hitchhiking. Miserably Jessica contemplated her fate—a fate almost equal to death. She still had no idea where she was going, but anything was better than Wonderlust. Anyplace that had never heard of latte was no place for Jessica Wakefield. Jessica knew if she could only get to a town with a skyscraper, she'd be in business. Civilization—with its cell phones, Aircon Service, and airports—would save her.

But you need to get there first! Jessica fanned her face with a menu she'd swiped from the karaoke bar, wishing she'd stolen a diet Coke too. Not a living soul anywhere in sight. And Jessica was starting to get creeped out. Though it was still morning, the sky was getting darker and the vacant expanse on either side of the asphalt was starting to work on her nerves. Wasn't this that weird UFO highway she'd heard about on *Dateline?* Route 66 or Highway 1 or whatever? *Or maybe it's that serial-killer highway,* she thought nervously. *Where that guy picks up women hitchhikers and decapitates them!* Her throat constricted in terror. She could already see the news report that would air after they'd found her bloody remains.

"Out here, no one can hear you scream," Maria Shriver would begin in a somber voice, holding up Jessica's bloodstained Laura Van Meulenmeister platform. "And in Jessica Wakefield's case, no one did hear. This pink shoe is all that's left!" Jessica's eyes widened in fear. *Like the Australian dingo and the baby!* she thought wildly, surveying the landscape with terror. Even if she did survive the serial predator, anything could leap out of the Badlands at any minute.

For all I know, the Children of the Corn live here, she thought gloomily as she trudged forward. *Maybe not corn,* she amended, taking in the bleakness of the dusty land. *But they could have cousins—Children of the Scrub!* Jessica stiffened. She wasn't sure, but she thought she caught movement out of the corner of her eye.

There was nowhere to hide. They were coming out, moving stealthily behind the rocks, their evil red eyes expressionless, their movements methodical.

Snap out of it, Jessica! She stopped walking and sat down right in the middle of the asphalt.

Obviously the heat and the exertion were making her hallucinate. "Get a grip, girl!" Saying the words out loud helped, and Jessica quickly felt in the pockets of her capri pants. She knew she desperately needed to put on a fresh face to the world, and thank goodness she had a compact and a lipstick with her. In her opinion, far more essential than water, even in the desert. *Because if you don't look good, why bother to live anyway?* Jessica reasoned, skimming her lips with a glossy color called Love That Fuchsia.

Bingo! Jessica snapped her compact closed and shot to her feet. Out of the dust she could just make out what appeared to be a big, fancy car coming toward her. *The miracles of pressed powder!* she thought in wonder. It was incredible, but the cliché, which her best friend, Lila Fowler, repeated like a mantra, was true: Makeup made things happen!

Jessica cocked her hip, licked her lips, and pouted, gunning for the Guess?-ad look: ravishing roadside babe in no-man's-land. She knew she could pull it off. Haughtily she stuck out her thumb as a fiery red Cadillac swam into focus. Bonus! A Caddy meant a guy at the wheel! And—double bonus! As the car slowed, she could see a high-cheekboned driver with a perfectly coiffed 'do. Hot rod and hot guy! Could it be a mirage?

"Hey, little lady. Need a ride?" the dark stranger drawled in a husky southern accent that made Jessica think of molasses and gravel mixed together. *Mirages don't speak!* she thought in excitement, her heart leaping like a Norwegian salmon in spring. With his pomaded, fifties-style jet-black pouf, slanted gray-green eyes, and spiffy, royal blue silk shirt, the suave stranger was the answer to Jessica's prayers. And then some. A rescuer—and an ultraswanky one to boot!

"I guess I do, mister," Jessica replied breathily, lowering her eyelashes demurely and almost unconsciously adding a cool, southern lilt to her voice. *Although I couldn't tell you where!* Not that it really mattered anymore. As the stranger got out of the car and Jessica's eyes flickered appreciatively over his long, lean physique and fitted-but-not-too-tight black dress pants, she already felt aeons away from Team One and all the bad memories she associated with the contest.

"Allow Elvis Presley to help you out, ma'am!" the stranger added, breaking into a grin that revealed flawless white teeth.

Jessica smiled and sashayed over to the Caddy. "I'd like that," she replied, her spirits lifting with every step. After all she'd been through since Neil's revelation last night, the studly stranger was exactly what she needed. Everything was going to be A-OK from now on. She felt sure of it. *I'm in safe hands,* Jessica reflected gratefully. *But hopefully not too safe!*

Chapter Two

"I just don't get how we managed to leave Jessica behind!" Tom muttered, shaking his head in disbelief. The news was still sinking in.

"If you think about it, you could answer your own question in a heartbeat!" Todd muttered in response. "At best, Jessica is a first-class ditz—and at worst, she has a teamwork threshold of minus five. Knowing her, the novelty of the trip wore off and she decided she needed to get back to her hairdresser!"

This is the last straw! Tom thought irritably, his head buzzing. Waking up with tequila soaking his brains was bad enough. And on top of that, he had to contend with the fact that it was Wilkins who'd gotten him there—his least favorite person on the team, even taking Jessica into account. Tom mentally cursed himself for getting so wasted with Wilkins. They'd spent half the evening acting like best buddies when it was no secret that neither one could stand the other.

Tom's skin prickled as Todd raised his voice and began to deliver his theories on what their next move should be. *He thinks he's such a natural-born leader!* Tom thought in disgust. And it wasn't just that Todd behaved like a pompous jackass whenever the occasion allowed, flexing mental and physical muscles to prove himself to the world. As if that kind of macho behavior weren't grating enough, Todd was Elizabeth's "other" guy, her high-school sweetheart—and the only person besides Tom that Elizabeth had ever loved.

At the thought of Elizabeth, Tom's chest tightened painfully. Although he and Elizabeth had called it quits a while ago, Tom still had a hard time letting her go. She was the one woman who really mattered—the only woman who ever really had. He still thought they deserved another shot at being together. *And I'm going to prove it to her!* Tom vowed, not for the first time. All through the trip he'd been trying to figure out ways to impress Elizabeth and show her he was still the guy for her.

But this latest turn of events seriously threatened Tom's chances. The matter of Jessica's disappearance would not exactly sit well with Elizabeth. *If she finds out her sister's been left behind, she's going to go ballistic!* Tom thought grimly, massaging his

30

aching head. So much for proving himself to Elizabeth. *Way to go, fool!* Tom cursed himself. He should have kept a closer eye on Jessica. But now it was too late. There was no way of minimizing the damage. They were hours and hours away from Wonderlust, South Dakota, and getting Jessica back would require some serious brainstorming.

"I knew she'd ditch us. She's been whining and complaining all through the trip," Rob exclaimed, shaking his head in disgust. "That girl is trouble!"

"There's no point in dwelling on that now," Todd boomed, holding up his hands. "We've got to think, and think fast."

Can't argue with that. Tom's eyes flickered over Todd's worried face. *We're in the same boat,* he acknowledged grimly. Todd knew Elizabeth as well as Tom did, and he also knew how furious she'd be if she discovered her twin was out there all by herself somewhere and that Tom and Todd were the ones who had let it happen.

"We're finished—and just when we were in the lead!" Pam wailed, clutching Rob's arm for support. "If we don't get Jessica back, the team will be disqualified in Missouri!"

"More to the point, we'll be nailed by Elizabeth for losing her twin sister," Tom muttered, thinking aloud.

"Yeah," Todd agreed. "Elizabeth is generally a calm person, but when she explodes, it's not a pretty scene."

31

We should have put a leash on Jessica's foot! Tom thought grimly. She could be anywhere by now, and there was no telling what kind of trouble she'd gotten herself into. They could only pray she was OK and was keeping her wits about her. But knowing Jessica, that was too much to ask. No, there was only one way out of the jam they were in. They'd have to go all out to get Jessica back before something disastrous happened to her. And that meant Tom would have to work with Todd, something he wasn't thrilled about, but knew was necessary.

"So, what are we going to do? We can't exactly go back for her. Wall or Wonderlust is what, four hours away?" Tom turned to Todd, who nodded bleakly in assent. "Maybe she's finding her way to us. . . ."

"Not likely." Todd began to pace the narrow kitchen area. "How should I put this? Jessica's—uh—geographically challenged. She doesn't even know how to unfold a map, much less follow one."

"Hey, guys, give her a break, would you?" Neil cut in sharply. "I'm sure Jessica didn't get left behind on purpose."

"I wouldn't put it past her!" Rob broke in angrily, pausing between sympathetic kisses to the top of Pam's head. "And now we're paying for it. If we go back to South Dakota, we'll have to stop at every rest stop and small town along the way

32

and we'll never make it to Lincoln by tomorrow morning."

"Yeah, but if Jessica doesn't make her way to us by tomorrow morning, we're automatically out of the event and we'll have a whole lot of people to answer to!" Todd retorted. "I say we have no choice but to go back to Wonderlust."

Tom had to agree that Todd's was the most sensible suggestion. There was no way they could go on to St. Joseph minus Jessica. And if they did, Tom knew he could kiss good-bye forever his chances of winning back Elizabeth.

But as everyone closed doors, switched seats, and prepared to head back to Wonderlust, South Dakota, it suddenly occurred to Tom that there was a problem with the strategy—and the problem was major. "Hold it," he said abruptly to Todd. "If we go back to South Dakota, we're going to drive straight by the camera crew. They'll never let us keep going without demanding to know what's up."

"You're right!" Todd groaned. "That ICSN guy Ned told me at the last stop they were going to hang out for a while. So they must be an hour or so behind. That's all we need. Those nosy TV people fishing for info and then broadcasting it to everyone in Missouri."

Darn! Tom felt like putting a fist through the windshield, and he bet Todd felt the same way. This was a no-win situation. There was no way of avoiding the camera crew if they turned back. And if the crew figured out the truth, it would spread to Elizabeth faster than a forest fire through a stand of dry pines. Juicy news like this was exactly what the crew was looking for to spice up the preevent TV specials.

"But we've got no choice, have we?" Todd groaned. "If you can come up with a better solution, be my guest. But I think we have to go back. And deal with the TV crew when we come to them. Make something up. Fake them out somehow."

Tom nodded curtly and inserted the keys into the ignition. As he pulled away from the shoulder and turned the Winnebago around, he felt his headache begin to pinch even worse than before despite his sunglasses. *Everything's going backward—literally!* he noted gloomily, dreading the long hours of driving that were before them. *It had better be worth it!*

Tom's mouth narrowed in anger as he reflected on all the trouble and worry Jessica had caused. *She'd better have a real good excuse for this stunt!* Tom thought, flattening the accelerator. He spurred himself on by picturing the lecture he'd give Jessica when they caught up to her. Then a voice of doubt nudged at his consciousness. *If you catch up to her . . .* Tom fought the voice from gnawing at him further, but like a painful splinter under the skin, it couldn't be dislodged very easily. Maybe they wouldn't find Jessica!

Nervously Tom pumped the gas and watched

the speedometer jump. They were going extremely fast, but maybe not fast enough. Because maybe it was already too late.

"A little Woolite and it's as good as new!" Charlie Hoffman sang brightly as she rinsed Elizabeth's coffee-stained sweater in the bathroom sink. Tucking a strand of her chin-length blond hair back into a butterfly barrette, Charlie regarded Elizabeth compassionately. She looked so uncharacteristically morose, sitting in the Winnebago kitchen, staring glumly out the window. She'd barely uttered a word since she'd run out of the North Platte rest stop, her sweater soaked with coffee and her cheeks red with the embarrassment of having been such a klutz in front of Sam.

"Counting telephone poles?" teased Ruby Travers gently, placing a hand on Elizabeth's shoulder, but Elizabeth merely shrugged and kept her eyes on the road. Charlie shot Ruby an empathetic look. Ruby wasn't having any more luck trying to cheer up Elizabeth than she was. It was tough watching Elizabeth—normally so positive and energetic—dragging her lip on account of Sam. And it was even tougher trying to get her to open up about her feelings toward him. But Charlie knew that as a friend, she should keep trying.

"Look, Liz," she began tentatively, "I know you feel like you made a fool of yourself in the rest stop, but you're magnifying this whole situation."

Ruby nodded in confirmation, sliding a Tupperware container of chocolate-pecan brownies toward Elizabeth. "It's not the end of the world."

"Definitely," Ruby said, nodding vigorously, her mane of thick, dark corkscrew curls bouncing with the movement. "And maybe it was a good thing you spilled the coffee. Divine intervention!" Ruby extended a delicate but well-muscled arm across the table and snatched a brownie. "You said you were about to confront Sam about last night and all. But that might have been even more disastrous than spilling the coffee. Maybe it was a sign," she finished, breaking her brownie into two halves.

"I agree," Charlie added as Elizabeth looked at her inquiringly. "Maybe it's better to leave Sam alone. Telling him to back off and stop acting so weird to you isn't necessarily the right way to deal with a guy like that," she went on. "Not that he's a jerk or anything," she added lamely, wishing Elizabeth didn't look so crestfallen.

The truth was, Charlie didn't really know how to make Elizabeth feel better about the situation with Sam. Part of the problem was Elizabeth's own caginess. Charlie knew that Elizabeth felt conflicted about Sam and that she'd had enough of his bad attitude. But Elizabeth had been enigmatic about the details of some of her conversations with Sam and continued to pretend there was nothing seriously romantic about their relationship. *Ha!* It was seriously obvious to Charlie that there were some pretty strong currents swirling beneath the surface of Elizabeth and Sam's so-called friendship. Especially after that kiss on the dance floor last night!

Something's definitely going on between them, Charlie mused, studying Elizabeth shrewdly. The whole team was aware that from day one Elizabeth and Sam seemed to rub each other the wrong way. Things were always charged between them, and their fights produced the kind of sparks that suggested romance masquerading as anger. They had the love-hate thing down pat, one day loathing each other, the next day sharing secret looks that both Charlie and Ruby, if not Josh and Uli, had noticed. *If only Liz would confide in me like I do with her,* Charlie thought.

"Thanks, guys, but this pep talk isn't really necessary," Elizabeth responded, breaking into Charlie's thoughts. "I don't really care what Sam thinks," she added tonelessly.

Charlie raised an eyebrow, and she and Ruby shared a look of mutual frustration. If Sam was causing Elizabeth this much pain, then why was Elizabeth wasting valuable time even thinking about the guy? Charlie couldn't figure it out. She was all for being nonjudgmental, but she had her own private opinions about Sam Burgess. Sure, he had the rebel James Dean thing going, but as far as Charlie was concerned, that kind of bad-boy cockiness worked better in the movies than in real life. Plus he'd been really mean to Charlie about her driving skills—or lack thereof.

Luckily I don't have to worry about that in my own relationship, Charlie thought with relief, twisting the antique ruby-and-gold ring she wore on her right index finger. A small smile played at her lips as she thought of her boyfriend, Scott, who'd given her the ring on Valentine's Day. Their relationship was as real as it got.

Scott was rock solid, a perfect, attentive boyfriend. Charlie only wished she could be with him now, but her conservative, control-freak parents had made sure that couldn't happen. Her face darkened into a scowl as she thought of her parents forcing her to go on the road trip to keep her and Scott apart for the summer. *"Too intense, too soon"*—Charlie could hear her parents' words ringing through her head. *But they can't stop us!* she thought with a secret smile. Nobody—with the exception of Elizabeth—knew it, but Scott had been following Team Two since they'd left San Francisco. He'd seen her last night in Wonderlust, South Dakota, and planned on meeting her again in only a few days. Charlie could hardly wait.

"Come on, Liz, you need that brownie!" Ruby said, nudging the Tupperware container even closer to Elizabeth. Elizabeth shook her head but managed a smile as Ruby plucked another brownie and promptly popped the entire square into her mouth. "Yum!" she exclaimed, brushing crumbs off her faded denim overalls. "How about you, Charlie?"

Charlie declined and tried not to make a face. The thought of eating a brownie made her feel nauseous, and she already felt carsick. In fact, for the last few days she'd been feeling fatigued and kind of weak. *It's all this driving!* Charlie thought, steeling herself against a wave of queasiness as the Winnebago glided around a corner.

"Are you OK, Charlie?" Ruby surveyed her warily. "All of a sudden you're looking a bit green around the gills."

"I'm fine," Charlie managed weakly, waving a hand as Elizabeth and Ruby both peered at her with concern. "It's only a little motion sickness. I'll just lie down for a while."

But back in her bunk, Charlie couldn't quite quell the anxiety churning and mixing with the bile in her stomach. *It'll all be over soon,* she told herself. *Only a few weeks and then you'll be home and back to your old self!* But the words rang hollowly in her head. She wasn't quite right. Charlie could feel it in her bones. She couldn't put her finger on it, but she knew something was wrong. She only hoped it was nothing serious.

"Oh, jeez! It's the camera crew!" Todd groaned. "Just keep going, Tom. We'll pretend we didn't see them."

"Yeah, right! They're only in a van the size of a fire truck, signaling like crazy for us to slow down," Tom snapped. "I told you this would happen."

No, doofus, I told you! Todd thought irritably, but he kept his words to himself. They had more immediate concerns to address. "Everybody, just act natural!" Todd hissed as they slowed to a stop and he, Tom, and Neil hopped out of the Winnebago.

"Hey!" Ned Jackson, Intense Coast-to-Coast's head field producer, waved as he loped toward them.

"This is just what we need," Neil muttered. "What now?"

"I'll ad-lib something," Todd said through a plastic smile. But his heart was pounding, and his brain was drawing blanks. *Just relax,* he ordered himself. The main thing was not to sound a red alert.

"So, what's up, guys? We thought you were miles ahead!" Ned regarded them shrewdly from beneath his orange Intense Cable Sports Network baseball cap.

"Just a minor detour," Todd said quickly. "We—ah—Jessica left her purse at the rest stop in North Platte."

"Yeah," Tom added. "You know Jessica. Always losing things. One of these days it'll be her mind," he joked weakly.

"So, we'll catch up with you guys later," Todd said casually. "We'd better get moving."

"Whoa! Wait a second!" Todd froze as Ned went on. "Are you guys for real? You're going to go all the way back to North Platte just to find Jessica's purse? Get outta here!" He cracked his gum and hooked his thumbs into the belt loops of his jeans.

Get off our backs, will you? Todd thought angrily. He wasn't exactly wild about Ned—or any of the camera crew, for that matter. They were always meddling, always playing the big guys and getting in everyone's way. Typical TV guys, in Todd's opinion, overestimating the importance of their jobs. And Ned had always struck Todd as kind of slow. *Unfortunately he picks now to get smart!* Todd thought. His head was ticking, but he had to play it cool or there would be trouble.

"Yeah, driving back is definitely a grind," he said, "but Jessica's such a prima donna. You know women," he added, shaking his head. "What can you do? It's crazy to drive all this way, but Jessica would drive us crazier if we didn't!" *Please let that be enough!* Todd prayed.

"Yeah, I know what you mean," Ned replied, a smile creasing his deeply tanned face. "Ladies. They'll drive us all crazy one day."

Bingo! Todd shot Tom and Neil a secret look of relief. *Now we can get this show back on the road.*

"This is a great opportunity," Ned mused, evidently

not yet ready to let them go. "I mean, this is real drama. Just the sort of behind-the-scenes action we need for the next biweekly broadcast. You know, *Coast-to-Coast Real Notes,* all about the nitty-gritty of the road trip, the day-to-day dramas, the ins and outs of the whole caper. . . ."

He can't be serious! Todd stifled a groan as Ned grew more and more animated with every triple-hyphenated description. "Guys, this is perfect!" Ned clapped and beamed. "Let me grab my camera, and we'll do a quick interview with Jessica!"

Todd shook his head and tried to look regretful. "No can do, Ned. I mean, it's a cool idea and everything; I can see the appeal—but I'm afraid Jessica won't."

"Definitely not," Neil interjected. "She's just way too upset about it. She feels like a real moron, and we've ragged on her enough as it is. I don't think she'll want to have her forgetfulness plastered all over the TV news. That's just not the way Jessica wants to be known."

"Well, no harm in asking," Ned replied, taking his camera from another crew member and turning toward the Winnebago. "Where is she?"

Cripes! Todd panicked as Tom shot out in front of Ned, blocking his way to the RV.

"Believe us, man, this is not a good idea!" Tom babbled. "She's feeling way too stressed. And I gotta warn you—Jessica Wakefield stressed out is not a pretty scene. Is it, Pam?" he yelled stagily to

Pam, who was leaning out the curtained side window of the Winnebago.

"Uh—yeah," Pam mumbled.

"Yeah! I mean, no!" Rob echoed weakly from inside the Winnebago.

"I just want to talk to her!" Ned replied irritably. "Jessica, are you in there?" he shouted.

Think, Wilkins! Use your nut! Todd knew that disaster was just around the corner. He had to come up with a quick save or the game would be over. "I'll talk to her. We'll talk to her," he amended, motioning to Tom. "We'll ask her if she wants to talk to you," he finished as Ned rolled his eyes. "C'mon, Tom, I think she's in back," he continued, edging toward the door of the Winnebago.

"What's your plan?" Tom muttered.

"Just get inside there and pretend to be Jessica!"

"What?" Tom shook his head as they climbed the stairs. "I'm not getting you."

Todd pulled Tom toward the back of the Winnebago. "I know it's dumb, but Ned won't quit unless we throw him something. You can do voices, right? So just fake it!"

"Are you kidding?" Pam hissed, turning away from the window. "If anyone should do Jessica, I should. She's female, for pete's sake!"

Todd and Tom shared a look that suggested they were thinking the exact same thing. Sure, Pam was a girl, but her voice was way too distinctive to be mistaken—more like chalk squeaking on a

43

blackboard than sounds from a human throat. No, the situation was dire, and there was neither time nor place for tact.

"Look, Pam, I'm sorry to break it to you, but your voice is—well, it's unmistakably your voice," Todd explained quietly.

"My voice?" Pam squeaked. "What's wrong with my voice?"

"Put a lid on it, Pam," Tom snapped briskly. "And let me in there . . ."

"So, where is she?" Ned demanded from just outside the Winnebago. "I've got the camera, and the sound guy's ready."

Todd appeared in the doorway and looked down at Ned. "She doesn't want to come out. She knows you're going to videotape her, and she isn't up for it." Todd shot Neil what he hoped was a re-assuring glance. Neil looked like he was ready to pass out with worry.

"It's just a one-minute interview, Jessica," Ned shouted. "These are the kinds of details the folks at home will want to see, the stuff they can relate to. You know, the little quirks that make you distinctly you!"

"Yeah, well, I don't feel like me right now!" Tom crooned in a perfect falsetto. Todd almost laughed out loud. Tom was brilliant, his voice a dead ringer for any teary eighteen-year-old girl's voice!

"Why don't you come outside and tell me all about it," Ned wheedled, trying to angle his camera into the window.

Suddenly the window cracked open a tiny bit farther and a pair of red-lipsticked lips quivered next to the glass. Tom in lipstick! It was almost more than Todd could bear. He stole a glance at Neil and saw that his face was red with suppressed laughter.

"Listen, Ned," the lips hissed, "I know you think your *Coast-to-Coast Real Notes* idea is a swell one, but allow me to give you a reality check: It's the lamest, most ludicrous notion this side of the equator, and believe you me, your so-called audience is about as interested in my pathetic little plot as I am in telling them about it. So go poke your camera in someone else's window because I am not—and I repeat, not—going to be fodder for you guys to make a fool of!"

Before Ned could respond, the window slammed shut.

"Whoa!" Ned lowered his camera and looked incredulously at Todd. "I see what you mean. She's some tough lady!"

"Ned, you have no idea!" Todd said as Ned stalked back to his van.

"Well, I guess we pulled that one off." Neil shook his head in disbelief. "We're still in the running."

But only just, Todd thought. As he climbed back into the Winnebago, he felt suddenly exhausted. It was true, they were still in the contest. But Jessica still had to be found—and time was running out.

Chapter
Three

It doesn't get wackier than this—an Elvis impersonator to the rescue! Jessica giggled, noting "Elvis's" blue suede shoes as he crossed over to her side of the car and opened the passenger door. "So what's your real name, stranger?" she cooed, flashing him a sultry gaze.

"Elvis Aaron Presley. I'm as real as it gets, honey!"

"Yeah, right! And I'm Marilyn Monroe!" Jessica shot back with a throaty chuckle.

"Hot damn! I thought I recognized that outfit—Marilyn!" the stranger replied, his eyes skimming lazily over Jessica's skimpy halter top and low-slung capris. "Haven't seen you in a while. How you been, sugar?"

This ought to be interesting! Jessica raised a perfectly plucked eyebrow as "Elvis" flashed her a seductive smile. Once in the Caddy, Jessica sat back in the deep, burgundy-leather passenger seat and

47

savored the situation. "Rock Around the Clock" on the car stereo and a smooth stud beside her. "So, you're really not going to give up your true name?" she added mischievously.

"Told you the first time, little lady. And the King never tells a lie. I'm a true blue!" Elvis replied, revving the car.

Make that very interesting! Obviously Elvis fully intended on keeping the joke rolling. And that was cool with Jessica. Especially since he really did look uncannily like the young Elvis, from the curled lip, to the coiffed hair, to the smoky eyes that could sizzle you with a glance. Even his voice sounded eerily like the King's.

"So, I'm headed back to Memphis. How 'bout you, darlin'?" Elvis asked as he guided the Caddy back onto the highway.

Jessica's face fell. "That's the million-dollar question." As she filled Elvis in on the details of her dilemma—naturally deleting the part about Neil's rejection—she felt a twinge of panic snake through her stomach.

"I'll take you anywhere you like, but maybe we should go back to Wonderlust first. Check and see if your people have come back for you."

"No way, Jose!" Jessica's reaction was instantaneous. "I refuse point-blank to go back to Wonderlust!" Just thinking about the ugly, genetically deprived bartender was revolting.

"Well, then, how 'bout Memphis with me, Ms.

Monroe? I can show you the sights, and then I'll take you wherever you need to be."

Jessica blushed as Elvis's gaze grazed her body with the lightness of fingertips. He truly was megaluscious. And his offer sounded pretty fab. Why bother with a plebeian college contest when she could be burning it up with a handsome stranger? *Especially since for all I know, they left me behind on purpose!* Jessica thought angrily. Still, she knew the whole team could be DQ'd if she didn't show. Or at the least they'd come in stone last. *And maybe they did go back for me,* she thought suddenly. *Maybe they're here in South Dakota right now!* Not likely, but possible.

But if Team Two had gone back for her and Jessica went back to meet them, she'd have to face Neil. That was an alarming thought. At best, he would be patronizing and fake, pretending he didn't think she was a total twerp. At worst, he'd treat her like she had bubonic plague. And Jessica knew she couldn't deal with either scenario. *Nor do you have to,* she told herself, perking up at the thought of tearing up Memphis with swanky Elvis by her side. Judging by the gleam in his eye, Elvis had big plans for just the sort of outrageous adventures that kept Jessica's pulse racing. The sort of adventures that would help her forget Neil even existed.

Neil who? Jessica's eyes lingered on Elvis's unbuttoned shirt collar, his pectoral perfection clearly visible from her angle. The amnesia was already setting in, and the trip hadn't even begun. . . .

But just as she drifted lazily into a Memphis daydream, Jessica's conscience pinpricked her fantasy bubble, making her feel like slime for considering ditching the team. Her eyes fluttered open and she sat up, irritated at the interruption. *Why couldn't I have left my conscience in the Winnebago instead of my purse!* she wondered, sighing. There was no getting away from it. Turning her back on the team would be a pretty shabby thing to do. Unless they turned their backs on her first!

Jessica bit her lip. She was at a crossroads. It was either turn back or ride off into the unknown.

"So, what'll it be?" Elvis prodded. "Your wish is my command."

Jessica swallowed. She had to make a choice. And either way, that choice would affect the rest of her summer.

"I could give you some advice," Elvis offered as Jessica shifted uncomfortably in her seat. "Just a little something I've picked up in my days as a musician."

"Well, spit it out, Presley. I could use a few words of wisdom. I could even use a cliché. I'll take whatever you've got!"

"Two things," Elvis began, leaning closer to Jessica. "Go where you're wanted, and follow your heart. In my experience they both pretty much amount to the same thing."

50

"Yeah, well, that doesn't help," Jessica snapped. "Every time I've followed my heart, I've ended up in a heap of dung. And as far as going where I'm wanted . . ." Jessica sighed airily. "I'm generally wanted in many places at once, by many people. That's just the way it's always been for me. Don't you have anything better?" she added wearily.

Elvis chuckled. "OK, honey," he said, his voice sobering. "This is a well-worn tidbit from my papa, and you can apply it to most any situation: Go with the flow."

"Huh?" Jessica screwed up her face in bewilderment. "That's not advice. That doesn't tell me anything! Maybe if I were a monk twiddling my thumbs in Tibet, I'd find that useful, but *here*? Now? Go with the flow? Puh-leeze!"

"Well . . ." Elvis narrowed his eyes in concentration. "Hear me out a second. I may be wrong, but it sounds to me like you've shredded your rope with the team already. You got left behind, deliberately or by accident, it doesn't matter. And maybe that's a sign you should move on. Follow the path you're on instead of trying to turn back and swim against the current."

Jessica had to admit Elvis had a point. But could she really justify bailing out altogether? "What about the competition?"

"I say take some time, figure things out. When and if you're ready to go back to your friends, I

51

can get you to wherever you need to go in half the speed of any Winnebago." Elvis smiled. "All I'm saying is, it doesn't have to be all or nothing. Just relax and see where the road takes you."

"Hmmm . . ." Jessica chewed her cheek and tapped the dash with her nails as she digested Elvis's advice. On the one hand, it made a lot of sense. On the other, it sounded like a crock.

Just make a decision! Jessica ordered herself impatiently. But even after a full minute of weighing the pros and cons, she still didn't know which way to go. All she knew was that she was an all-or-nothing person and didn't do things in half measures. She would either go back or move on, but she would make her choice and stick to it.

For better or worse, there would be no turning back.

"We're finally here!" Ruby exclaimed. Elizabeth stifled a yawn as she stumbled out of the Winnebago and looked around her. They'd parked at Wagon Train Lake Campground on the outskirts of Lincoln, and the peaceful scene helped settle her nerves. A day of bumpy roads, spilled coffee, and avoiding Sam was more than enough stress, and she welcomed the sight of the small lake, a willow tree trembling at the edge of the water.

Team Four was already there. Elizabeth waved at her SVU friends Danny Wyatt and Alisha Korn but went down to the water immediately rather than joining in the excited chatter of the two teams. She wasn't in the mood for crowds, especially one Sam was a part of. There he was, laughing boisterously with Josh and with Mickey James from Team Four and making a big show of greeting Team Four's Vickie Dupont, a cool blonde whose always perfect hair and makeup irked Elizabeth almost as much as the way at every opportunity Vickie hung all over Sam and praised him in syrupy tones. *Just what he needs—more ego stroking!* Elizabeth thought bitterly, moving farther along the lake's edge to sit on a rock.

"Too noisy for you too?"

Elizabeth was startled, but she smiled and made room for Ruby on the wide slab of slate.

"How about something moody," Elizabeth said as Ruby lifted her guitar into her lap. As the soft but mournful sounds of a minor chord reached her ears, Elizabeth closed her eyes and allowed herself to be transported by Ruby's mellow voice singing about the melancholy of Sunday evenings.

As the song ended, Elizabeth squeezed her friend's arm. Ruby seemed to be getting better and better every day.

"How do you do that?" Elizabeth said slowly. "Make up a song out of nothing, I mean."

"It's hard to explain," Ruby replied as they stared out across the flat expanse of water. "I can't

53

exactly describe it, but it has to do with opening your mind and clearing it, and then channeling all your energy and somehow hoping it will lead to something. There's a lot of improvising," she added.

"No wonder I don't write songs!" Elizabeth rested her chin on her knees and sighed. "I'm hopeless at anything that doesn't have a clear path. I guess I just lack the power of imagination."

"Hey, don't knock yourself. Maybe you just haven't really tried," Ruby offered kindly. "It's all about tapping into different processes, opening yourself up to different possibilities."

Unless you're boring like me! Elizabeth picked up a pebble and skimmed it across the surface of the lake. Sometimes when she talked to Ruby, she felt dull and mechanical by comparison. Ruby was such a free spirit, carving out her own idiosyncratic, creative ideas without caring what anyone else thought. Elizabeth, on the other hand, had always followed a conservative path, doing what she felt she should, fussing over grades and midterms and obsessing over her professional future.

"I guess I see my songs like I see my life," Ruby continued, tossing a pebble into the lake. "To me, everything is a series of circles—like that ripple out there. I've never seen myself as being the sort of person that can follow a straight line. You know, go to college, graduate, climb the next rung on the social ladder. Maybe I'm crazy, but I think sometimes you have to throw the pebble randomly and just see how it falls."

"I don't think you're crazy," Elizabeth replied quietly. And although Elizabeth had initially resisted Ruby's philosophy, discouraging her from dropping out of school and hitting the road with her guitar, she was beginning to wonder if maybe she wasn't the one in need of guidance. *Maybe I'm too traditional and narrow-minded,* she wondered. *And maybe I'm missing out somehow!*

As Elizabeth shared her fears with Ruby, she found herself feeling calmer and more centered than she'd felt in weeks. Ruby really seemed to understand her, and her words were simple and comforting, smoothing away some of the tension Elizabeth felt inside.

"The thing is, if you have these really specific expectations and goals, then everything suddenly becomes weighted," Ruby explained. "And then everything has to conform to your expectations or else you end up disappointed."

Elizabeth nodded glumly. That was precisely what was happening in her life. She was so busy keeping on her track, expecting everything to fit into the space she had designated for it, that she didn't know how to react when something—or someone—came out of left field. Like Sam.

If my life is a big jigsaw puzzle, then Sam's the piece that won't fit! Elizabeth acknowledged. But maybe, as Ruby suggested, the problem lay with

Elizabeth, with her ruthless expectations and fixation on organizing everything to be just so. *There's no room for improvisation and spontaneity in my life,* Elizabeth realized as her eyes caught the path of two dragonflies tracing circles just above the water.

"Liz, maybe you just force things too much," Ruby suggested. "Maybe it's time to let life happen rather than expect everything to happen according to your plan."

Elizabeth nodded as the dragonflies dipped in and out, making a crazy pattern in the air. Ruby—and the dragonflies—made a lot of sense. Maybe it was time to let things roll, to let the pieces fall however they chose. And that applied to Sam too.

"Sometimes you just need to let go and stop trying to control your universe," Ruby finished. Elizabeth nodded and stood up. She had a lot to mull over now, but she needed to do it alone. Because if she followed Ruby's advice, that would mean letting go of Sam and leaving it up to fate to decide their future. And although Elizabeth could see the wisdom in the idea, there was danger in it too. *Because sometimes when you let a person go,* she thought, *they're gone forever.* And Elizabeth didn't know if "forever" was a risk she was willing to take.

Now this is what it means to be on the road! Jessica thought gleefully, a thrill of excitement electrifying her skin as the Cadillac zoomed down the highway. She felt totally, one hundred percent alive and opened her arms wide, savoring the wind on her body. *As carefree as a model in a Double-mint ad!* she thought with the smile of satisfaction that went with knowing she looked as sexy and invigorated as she felt.

Nothing gave Jessica more pleasure than being the focal point of an aesthetically pleasing image, and being in a sleek car with a sleek guy was as good as it got. Especially since that sleek guy had also turned out to be a generous one, buying Jessica as many changes of clothes as she needed from what seemed the only boutique in the heartland—some down-and-out discount store in Goodness-knows-where. Of course, Jessica had only managed to stomach buying two el cheapo, body-hugging Lycra dresses and a pack of Hanes for Kids tees—for the cutoff, figure-hugging look. Not exactly haute couture, but she knew she could make it work. And bad threads were a small price to pay for being rid of the team.

Team One, eat dirt! As the Caddy bulleted toward the horizon, Jessica couldn't believe she'd spent more than twelve seconds thinking about her tedious teammates. After all, Neil was the only one she hadn't found utterly odious, and with each mile she put between them, the picture had become clearer and more distant at the same time: Obviously Neil had ditched her, either with or without the help of the team. The details didn't matter. All that mattered was that she'd made the right choice. *Like there'd even been a choice!* Jessica shook her head in wonder, picturing herself lumbering down the interstate in a lowly, unattractive Winnebago instead of zipping along in Elvis's hot rod. Hello? What had she been thinking?

Jessica shook her head, clearing all loathsome thoughts and memories of nasty, team-oriented road trips from her mind. Thankfully, she had come to her senses and gotten back in touch with who she really was and who she most definitely was not—namely, some map-reading, baseball-cap-wearing team trooper. That sort of nonsense was invented purely for the "infotainment" of the unsophisticated peons who made up the student body of the four competing schools. But Jessica Wakefield was meant for bigger and better things—exciting, spontaneous, maybe even dangerous things. And she had no doubt she was well on her way.

I'll take Memphis! she gloated, a delicious tickle of anticipation working its way up her spine. Jessica had no idea what Memphis was all about, but with Elvis by her side, she had no doubt it would be a blast.

"Step on it, E. I want to put a gazillion miles between us and those two-faced teamsters of mine!" she yelled above the engine's roar, but Elvis slowed as they approached a Mobil Stop-N-Go rest station.

"Sorry, Marilyn, but even a pretty lady like you can't keep this engine running when it's on empty. We need gas!"

As Elvis pulled into the rest stop, Jessica extended her legs over the door and out the window, ready for the admiring glances of weary travelers. These were the sorts of precious moments she treasured. Luckily there were plenty of cars around, which meant plenty of envious glances in her direction. *They'll probably wonder if we're doing a film together,* Jessica daydreamed, picturing the incredulous looks and hushed whispers of the local peasants as they spotted an Elvis and a Marilyn look-alike. Given the terrain, Jessica doubted the folks would even know that both Marilyn and Elvis were currently pushing up daisies. It would be safe to bet that at least one or two would mistake Elvis and Marilyn for real. And Jessica relished the prospect.

"Did you say your friends were driving a mustard-colored Winnebago?" Elvis queried, bursting Jessica's blissful fantasy.

"Vomit colored is what I said," Jessica replied crossly, irritated at having been so rudely interrupted. "Why do you have to bring up such a gross subject?"

"Because I think I see a group of people that matches your description. Right over there." Elvis pointed at the rest stop across the highway.

This has to be a bad dream! Jessica thought in

disbelief. She blinked and looked again, but there was no mistaking them: Neil, clearly visible in his favorite Stanford sweatshirt. Todd, pumping gas, his mirrored sunglasses reflecting across the asphalt. And the frizzy redhead could be none other than Pam. Even across the highway Jessica could hear her squawking like a chicken on steroids.

Well, well, well! Apparently they hadn't yet spotted Jessica, but that would all change very soon. Just looking at the team made Jessica's blood boil, and she could feel a surge of fury rushing up from the soles of her bare feet to the roots of her hair. They would be hearing from her. And they would get what they deserved for dumping her in that tacky karaoke bar!

And if you think you're coming back for me now, you've got another thing coming! Jessica seethed. It was all very well for them to blithely drive back for her when they'd decided, half a day later, that they needed her. But it was too late. And they would soon find that out!

Chapter
Four

This is my kind of lifestyle! Sam's eyes rested on the pink-orange sun, which seemed to hang almost precariously low in the sky. Things couldn't be more laid-back—Sam's favorite Beck CD providing a cool sound track to the scene, everybody chilling out nearby, and the lake, a postcard view, flat as a mirror and fringed with trees.

But something was off, and no amount of gold-flecked sky could make Sam fully appreciate the evening. He tried to pay attention to the chicken wings he was in charge of barbecuing, but his mind kept wandering back to Elizabeth, who was sitting not ten feet away on a picnic blanket. She hadn't turned to look at him once.

You could have let her down easier, Sam berated himself, picturing Elizabeth's face, pinched with hurt, when he'd told her he had a girlfriend in the Keys. Not that she was exactly a real girlfriend.

Sam had spun the situation so that both Josh and Elizabeth would understand he wasn't the kind of guy to be tied down to any one woman. He'd made it perfectly clear that his relationship with Angelina was a casual, no-promises kind of deal. The sort of thing that Sam was used to. The sort of thing he liked. And definitely not the sort of relationship he knew Elizabeth Wakefield would be up for. *Casual* was not a word girls like Elizabeth understood, and anything more was, well, too much for Sam.

Elizabeth was not only the sort of girl who made you stop and take notice, but also the sort that made you want to put on your sneakers and bail. Apart from being mind-spinningly gorgeous, she was mature and smart and all of the things that Sam knew he would want eventually in a woman. But now? He didn't think he could cut it. With girls like Elizabeth, there were no half measures. And just the pressure of knowing that Elizabeth had expectations of him brought out the jerk in Sam, somehow making him want to grab five beers and a random trashy girl and act as if he was a fifteen-year-old at the junior prom.

Scowling, Sam poked at the coals in the Weber, remembering the extremely hot kisses they'd shared the night before and then how he'd purposely ignored her this morning. *Maybe you just can't take the heat!* he thought grimly, stabbing a chicken wing with a skewer. All signs certainly pointed in that direction. And maybe it was time to get real, realize that no matter what potential he and Elizabeth might have five years down the line, right here and right now he wasn't able to deliver and she should quit hoping.

"You look like you could be using some company. Either that or a swim."

Sam chuckled and turned to see Uli, the tall, wiry Swede toweling off from a dip in the lake.

"Hey!" Sam cheered, clapping his friend on the back. Of all the guys on the road trip, Uli was definitely the one Sam connected with most. They were very different people, but they seemed to appreciate each other's differences.

"So, how about it, slacker?" Uli grinned and inclined his head toward the lake. "It is not very, very cold, you know," he teased.

"Not if you're used to swimming in fjords," Sam quipped. "Nah," he added. "Just don't feel like it tonight. Maybe tomorrow morning."

"So, what is up? You look like your head is hurting you." Uli narrowed his ice blue eyes. "You have some kind of heart trouble I should know about? Because you have that look."

"Oh yeah? What are you, Lundstrom, my personal shrink?" Sam grinned and shook his head. It was weird, but now and again Uli's unique brand of English described it best.

As Sam's eyes traveled back to Elizabeth, her blond hair spilling down her back, he felt something

63

kick inside him. He flicked his eyes back to Uli. No doubt Uli had seen—or at least heard about—Sam's passionate dance-floor moment with Elizabeth. Still, Sam hadn't told anyone about his conflicted feelings for Elizabeth. Even though he usually preferred not to talk about this kind of stuff, he wondered whether he should make an exception in this case. Run the scenario by his buddy. Uli was bound to have a different take on the situation, even if he couldn't offer any solid advice. *Might as well give it a shot,* Sam reckoned. Another look at Elizabeth—firmly and obviously ignoring him—confirmed that he had nothing left to lose. *You've probably lost it already,* he thought darkly as he took a deep breath and prepared to bring up the subject.

"Hey, guys!" Sam's admission was cut short by Josh, chewing on a piece of corn. "Need any brewskis over here?"

"No, thanks," Sam responded cheerfully, wishing Josh would disappear. The guy was OK, but he didn't have a sensitive bone in his body—and he always seemed to turn up at just the wrong moments.

"So, what are we talking about?" Josh tossed the eaten corn cob, grabbed a chicken wing off the barbecue, and blew on it.

"Sam's girlfriend," Uli joked.

"All the many, you mean!" Josh boomed, slapping Sam on the back. "Lover boy here has a girl in every port, you know," he continued loudly. "Florida—maybe even Stockholm!"

64

It was possible he imagined it . . . but Sam thought he saw Elizabeth stiffen. And then she got up and left the picnic blanket. She had heard! Mentally Sam cursed Josh for being so loud. If Elizabeth had had any doubts that he was a total loser, Josh's comments would pretty much have settled the question.

Oh, well, guess there's nothing more to figure out, Sam thought bitterly. It was too late. Sam tightened his jaw and mechanically turned over the burning chicken wings one by one. Maybe it was better this way. If Elizabeth hated him, the pressure would be off. Which meant no one would be disappointed when he failed.

"OK, Tom, have a look at this!" Todd demanded, flourishing a red marker and holding up the map.

"I don't need to look at the map! I have that thing engraved onto my brain! I know where we're going," Tom griped, rolling his eyes and whipping the map from Todd's hands. "Why don't you go stretch your legs, Wilkins," he added. "Looks like you need to blow off steam."

"Look who's talking!"

Ignoring Todd, Tom walked around the gas pump and stared at the double doors of the rest-stop restaurant. How long did it take to get a couple of snacks? Tom bet that Pam and Rob had conveniently forgotten the clock and were smooching it up all over the restaurant's Formica tables. The two were shameless.

So much for being on the road, Tom thought resentfully. He'd expected so much from the Coast-to-Coast trip, but now it looked as if he'd wind up with nothing—nothing but the agonizing daily grind of dealing with the team, and nothing to look forward to but Elizabeth's full-scale fury over their letting Jessica disappear. Not exactly the outcome he was after.

Boy, was I wrong—and so was Jack Kerouac! Tom shook his head in disgust. Maybe he had been a little idealistic, picturing the road trip as something wild and fun, a page out of a Beat generation novel or a scene from some crazy sixties movie. But somehow everything had gone backward, and instead of feeling free and spirited, Tom felt as if he were carrying a ten-ton garbage truck on his shoulders. The possibility of working things out with Elizabeth seemed as far removed as the possibility of finding Jessica. And everything else was just a painful waste of time.

Thinking of Jessica only made Tom feel even more bitter. If it wasn't for her, maybe things would be on track. But Jessica was a firecracker, and you never knew when she'd explode, leaving chaos in her wake. Which was exactly what she had done.

I'll bet she doesn't even care! Tom fumed, looking out across the highway. Knowing Jessica, she was probably hooked up with a rock star in a hot rod, burning rubber without a care in the world. *And causing trouble with everyone*, Tom hypothesized, watching a blonde at the rest stop across the freeway, engaged in what seemed like a hot-blooded conversation with a guy who was trying to placate her. The girl was a Jessica type, all right, right down to the hand gestures. . . .

Wait a minute! Tom craned his neck for a better look, shock scissoring through his stomach. Could it be?

Suddenly the blonde snapped her head around. Tom could see her mouth twisting angrily as she stared him down and stalked closer to the road to get a better look at him. There could be no doubt.

"Guys!" Tom hollered, elated at the sight of Jessica despite her obviously lousy mood. "We've found her. Hey, Jess!" he yelled. "We've found you!"

"Not for long!" Jessica shouted back. "It's a little late for reunions!"

"Jess, wait!" Neil ran up beside Tom. "Get over here! We need to talk!" he yelled as Jessica climbed into the waiting convertible.

"I don't think so!" Jessica hollered in response, tossing her hair. "Save your breath for someone else!"

"Jessica, we've been looking for you!" Tom pleaded, but Jessica only shook her fist at him.

"Forget about it!" she yelled. "You forgot me

once, it shouldn't be hard to forget me again!" she cried just before the car screeched down toward the exit.

"Everybody, let's move!" Todd bellowed as Neil rushed into the restaurant to find Pam and Rob. "We've got to get her back!"

If we can, Tom thought despondently as he watched the Cadillac speeding down the freeway. Suddenly he felt a sickly cocktail of anger and confusion sloshing through his insides and he exploded, opening his hand and smacking the side of a concrete pillar. *What is she on?* He couldn't fathom Jessica's strange attitude. After all, she'd caused all this pandemonium. But she was acting as if everyone else was to blame! Not that Tom should be surprised. He'd known Jessica long enough to be alerted to her arrogance. She never took responsibility for anything, even—and especially—when she'd single-handedly caused the problem.

She's going to hear from me! Tom vowed, his face thunderous as he marched back to the Winnebago. One way or another, they would catch up to Jessica. And she would get the mouthful she deserved. He would make sure of it.

"Oh yeah," Ruby murmured as she watched two fireflies tangoing above the lake. "I could definitely get used to this." Elizabeth and Charlie smiled and nodded in agreement.

But Ruby had really meant what she said. Although the others obviously appreciated the bohemian existence they were temporarily leading, Ruby knew their real lives would beckon them back—boyfriends, school, jobs, possessions. But Ruby was different, and as she abstractly plucked at her guitar strings, she wondered what, exactly, lay in her future.

It's all very well giving Liz advice, she thought ruefully, *but face it. Your life is one big, indecisive moment!*

Sighing, Ruby adjusted the embroidered guitar strap on her shoulder, a gift from a Brazilian friend who'd first introduced her to the guitar and who was now a major-label recording artist. As she fiddled for another pick in the pocket of her faded overalls, Ruby considered her choices for the millionth time. If she went back to school, she would be denying herself the chance to make it as a musician. But if she went on the road and tried to cut it on her own, she might fail miserably—and regret not having stayed in school. *"You need something to fall back on. . . ."* Ruby could hear her parents' words over and over like a mantra in her head. And she began to hear a tune to go with them.

"Something to fall back on," she sang, hesitantly at first, but gaining in strength as a more assured tune began to piece itself together—almost without her even trying. The words tumbled out, and Ruby found herself stringing together all the things she felt most anxious about. She was at a fork in the road. In fact, the whole road trip was starting to seem like a metaphor for her life, every confusing map and missed turn a sign of something deeper.

"Take a turn, live and learn, even if you lose," Ruby sang breathily, switching into a lower key. "These wide-open spaces, open places in my heart, like an old, forgotten letter lost in moments long since past."

The song was really starting to fly—Ruby could feel it. And as she went with the flow, the sentences stopped forming and the song became more like a collage, words jumbling together in a weird mix that didn't make sense in the usual way—but that made perfect sense because they mirrored the confusion she was trying to express.

"Wow!" Charlie whispered when the song faded into stillness.

"Strange, but—it worked," Elizabeth mused. "I think you've hit a groove, Ruby. That song's your best yet."

Ruby glowed with pleasure. Elizabeth just might be right. As she laid her guitar down on the grass, something in her stirred and then just as quickly settled. Ruby hugged her knees and looked out into the sky. Obviously this lifestyle was working out for her because she'd never felt stronger about her music. And maybe that was the signal she'd been waiting for, what she'd needed to set her free. After all, like that old saying of her grandmother's, Ruby just knew that a caged songbird never sings.

"I'll drive!" said Neil tersely, ousting Todd from the driver's seat. Todd scuttled out of the way, looking surprised at Neil's uncharacteristically determined manner, but Neil didn't pay him any attention. All he could think of was getting Jessica back.

Neil revved the engine and swerved the Winnebago out onto the open road with a screech of tires. He gripped the steering wheel as if it were a buoy and he a drowning man. This situation was getting way out of hand. He had to catch up with Jessica, and they had to straighten things out. That was all there was to it. Maybe she'd taken his kiss during that truth-or-dare game seriously? Whatever. Something about his behavior had given her the impression he liked her as a woman, and somehow Neil had to make up for that terrible misunderstanding.

"She's such a little diva!" Rob exclaimed angrily from the back. "I mean, what was that performance all about?"

"Just Jessica being a soap-opera queen," Todd replied nastily. "In her self-righteous little brain, she's managed to twist this whole situation around to make us into the villains. I swear, if we didn't have to get her back to save our own skins, I'd be only too happy to let her go."

"Whoa, you guys. Careful! Let's not get out of

hand here," Neil said, watching the speck on the horizon that was Jessica and her runaway car. He didn't like the way the conversation was going. Although he could understand the team's reaction to Jessica's latest stunt, he also thought that they were slamming her without really knowing what was going on. Jessica was out of line and behaving childishly, but only Neil knew that he wasn't blameless either.

"I don't think we're being out of hand," Tom responded. "You saw that display just now, Neil. What possible, reasonable explanation could there be for her behavior?"

Think fast! Neil commanded himself, feeling his hands grow clammy. How could he explain the fight and Jessica's stalking off? Everyone knew he and Jessica were exclusive members in a mutual admiration society. The other team members wouldn't just buy the excuse of a "fight" without wanting to know every detail. He couldn't tell them the truth. But he couldn't let the team rag on Jessica so badly either. *You have to defend her!* he told himself. But how could he without implicating himself? *It's a catch-22,* he thought miserably, his stomach churning.

"Look, guys," he began tentatively, "give Jess a little more credit. She's obviously upset because she thinks we ditched her. And we feel she ditched us. Somehow we all crossed wires. It's just a big misunderstanding."

"Yeah? Well, when we find her, Jessica had better have a very, very good explanation for this 'misunderstanding'!" Todd boomed in anger.

Oh no . . . Neil's face clouded in alarm as Todd's words rang in his ears. *What if we find her and she does give an explanation? The real, honest explanation? What if Jessica is so bitter about my having hurt her, she takes revenge by spilling my secret? But Jessica wouldn't do that! Or would she?* The thought hadn't occurred to Neil before, but now he felt a black cloud of helplessness descending on him like a sudden summer storm. Now he saw that the situation could actually get worse. He had to find a way to circumvent serious damage before it started.

There's only one way around that, Neil decided. *I have to find Jessica and talk to her before the others do. Make things OK between us. . . .* Neil's thoughts swirled around and around as he tried to imagine the logistics of the problem. It was only when they crested a hill and arrived at a fork in the road that he realized how futile it all was. *Too little, too late,* Neil thought hollowly as he brought the Winnebago to a grinding stop. There was no sign of Jessica. They had lost her.

"We can forget it now," Todd said dejectedly. "They were miles ahead of us, and it's a big country out there."

Neil put his head down on the steering wheel. Todd was right. It was hopeless. No one had seen which road Jessica had taken. Jessica was gone. And so was Neil's hope of working things out with her. Not to mention the team's chances at placing in the competition.

Neil couldn't help the slicing pain of disappointment running through his insides. With Stanford tuition through the roof, the first prize of five grand in scholarship money was nothing to sniff at. It had been his main incentive for taking the road trip in the first place. *But I can kiss that scholarship goodbye—along with Jessica,* he reflected mournfully.

"Maybe she just needs a few days," Tom suggested in a falsely hopeful tone of voice. "Jess is so impulsive. Maybe she'll skip this event but make it in time for the next. Her moods change with the weather," he continued weakly. But Neil knew that no one, least of all Tom, really believed they could wave a magic wand and have Jessica skip back into their lives in a few days.

"Oh, this is just pathetically awful!" Pam whined, tearing up and burying her head in Rob's chest. "Now we're hours away from where we're supposed to be, and it's all Jessica's fault!"

Not quite, Neil added silently. For the hundredth time the image of Jessica's hurt face twisting away from him the night before flashed through Neil's mind. And for the hundredth time he wished he could push a reset button and do the scene again. But he couldn't. He couldn't change what had happened.

His guilt—like his sexual orientation—had to remain a secret. Or he'd risk losing everything.

"I think that's them!" Elizabeth said to Ruby. She craned her neck to get a better look across the jam-packed St. Joseph town hall, but her hopes plummeted when she realized the guys she'd mistaken for Tom and Todd were just random cameramen.

Where are they? Elizabeth fretted, toying with her paper plate of breakfast muffins. She hadn't seen Team One since Sunday night, and it was now Thursday morning, the fourth event not twenty-four hours away.

Elizabeth was doing her best not to get flustered or jump to conclusions, trying valiantly to put Ruby's "path of least resistance" to the test, but she couldn't shake the nagging feeling that something was up. Her twin's sixth sense told her so, and when she got this feeling—a gut instinct she couldn't put into words—she was almost always proved right.

"Don't worry so much," Ruby advised, helping herself to a cup of herbal tea. "Jessica's in capable hands. And knowing her, she probably just convinced the team to take a detour. Anyway," she added, pausing to adjust the silver Mexican barrette that was keeping her thick ponytail from springing free, "there was no rule that everyone had to camp out at Wagon Train Lake."

"But no one's seen them in four days," Elizabeth replied edgily. She scanned the crowd, scrutinizing each face anxiously. It was hard not to panic when it was clear that all the other teams were present and accounted for. Nobody had chosen to skip the preevent breakfast—even the mayor of St. Joseph was there, as well as a reporter for the *Missouri Times* and WXFU, the St. Joseph community radio station. As she watched Team Three's competitive and snotty Alison Quinn kissing up to the mayor and trying to overstate her achievements to the journalists, Elizabeth felt Jessica's absence even more strongly. Alison was vice president of Jessica's sorority, Theta Alpha Theta, and one of Jessica's least favorite people. Jessica should be here, scoffing at Alison and sucking up all the press she could get. Jessica loved these preening opportunities, and Elizabeth was growing more and more suspicious.

"If I were you, I'd wait awhile before getting too worked up," Ruby suggested reasonably. "I'll bet you anything they'll be here in time for the cookout tonight."

"You're probably right." Elizabeth broke off a piece of banana-bran muffin and tried to dismiss her concern. There was plenty of time before the cookout, which meant plenty of time for Team One to arrive. Which meant plenty of time for her to worry!

Elizabeth bit her lip. It was pointless trying to calm herself down when the sense that all was not as it should be had begun to swell inside her, becoming more and more tangible and more and more urgent. *Please get here soon,* she prayed, hoping the disconcerting feeling would turn out to be nothing more than overreaction. But somehow she doubted it. Trouble seemed to follow Jessica like a faithful terrier. *And I'll bet anything that terrier is nipping at her heels right now!*

"Psst! Danny! Over here!" Tom popped his head out from behind a tree trunk, hoping he wouldn't have to shout any louder to get his friend to notice him. But Danny hadn't heard him. He was busy helping himself from the gigantic bowls of potato salad, trays of barbecued chicken, and immense platters of mixed green salads standing on rickety outdoor tables in the field behind St. Joseph's Shady Park Camp.

"Danny Wyatt!" Tom yelled hoarsely, ducking as he spotted Charlie and Ruby roasting marshmallows over a central fire pit. Elizabeth couldn't be far off, and Tom wanted to keep well hidden.

Danny whipped around and smiled when he saw his best friend. "Hey, man, I thought you'd never get here! What's up?" he exclaimed, joining Tom. "What are you hiding out for?"

"I'll tell you later." Tom looked fearfully around him. "Look, I just wanted to tell you that we're here in case Liz is freaking out. But I gotta lie low, and so does the rest of the team."

Danny frowned. "Why? What's the problem?"

"Later!" Tom hissed as a bead of perspiration prickled at his brow. The Jessica disaster had him so on edge, he felt as if he were hanging from a cliff by a human hair. After losing Jessica at the crossroad, things had gone from bad to worse. Exhausted and bickering over what to do next, they'd managed to get themselves lost again—resulting in several more exhausting days of driving.

We're lucky we even made it here at all! Tom thought bleakly. Everything was unraveling, and Tom could only hope to stall the inevitable run-in with Elizabeth until morning, when, he hoped, after a night of uninterrupted sleep he'd be more equipped to deal with her. *Not exactly a plan!* Tom thought grimly, but no one had come up with a better one. The rest of the team were still in the Winnebago, in the hopes that Jessica would suddenly turn up. Yeah, right! Tom knew that possibility was about as remote as their chances of even placing in the competition. And Elizabeth would have his head on a plate for it, meaning that any slight hope of getting her back would instantly dissolve into a big, fat zero. The best Tom could hope for was to avoid Elizabeth altogether and buy some more time.

"Listen, just tell Liz that everything's cool and that we're all getting an early night," he instructed, grabbing a bread roll from Danny's plate. "I gotta split!"

"Not so fast!" Tom wheeled around, groaning inwardly at the voice he knew so well. Elizabeth! "You only just got here? I came this close to sending out a search party!" she added.

So much for buying time. Attempting a reassuring smile, Tom tried not to look Elizabeth too closely in the eye. Her inquiring gaze and tapping foot told him all he needed to know. She expected answers, and they had to be believable.

"This is great. Comradeship between teams. Roll camera!" Ned Jackson! The meddling field producer clamped a meaty hand on Tom's shoulder and pushed him toward Elizabeth. "Just carry on with your reunion," he sang out cheerfully. "Act natural. You know the drill!"

I know I'm dead, and you want to bury me! Tom shot Ned a savage look and wished he could punch him squarely in his nicotine-stained teeth for his lousy sense of timing. But this was not the time and definitely not the place to act out. The Intense cameras were tracking his every move, and worse, Elizabeth was waiting.

79

"Maybe Ned already told you, Elizabeth . . ." Tom began to spin what he hoped was a convincing story centering around Jessica's lost purse. As he spoke, his voice gained in confidence and his body relaxed. Maybe the presence of the TV crew was actually helping. His WSVU broadcast experience had taught him how to be calm on camera. . . . "Of course, once we found the purse, our real troubles had only just begun," he continued. "Then Todd made us take a 'shortcut,' resulting in even more delays. Luckily I got us back on track in the end," he finished proudly. "Between Jessica and the rest of the team, it's been one crisis after the next!"

"Where is Jessica?" Elizabeth said impatiently.

"Uh, you didn't see her?" Tom feigned surprise. "Oh yeah, I guess she decided to hit the sack early. She's been clashing with Todd since we got lost, and I think she's pretty worn out."

"Speak of the devil!" Elizabeth waved at Todd, who was trying to sneak around a tree. *What's he doing here?* Tom panicked and shot Todd a thunderous look. *He was supposed to stay in the Winnebago. But no. He always has to be a part of the action. Control freak!* Tom thought irritably as the cameras panned to catch Todd and Elizabeth's friendly embrace.

"Hey, Liz. Tom." Todd looked cheerful enough. Maybe he'd just heard some good news? Tom knew he shouldn't hope, but maybe Jessica had decided to come back and Todd had come to let him know. A last-minute reprieve? Not likely, but with Jessica, Tom had come to expect the unexpected.

"So, Jess is already asleep, I hear?" Elizabeth asked skeptically.

"Out like a light," Todd replied smoothly. *At least he's quick on the uptake,* Tom thought grudgingly. He had to give the guy points for presence of mind, even if he was a pain in the neck.

"Oh yeah, well, Jess was really bummed at not finding her purse and totally worn out from arguing with Tom. He really put her through the wringer for her mistake," Todd added slyly. "Anyway, I told her to get a good night's sleep and that everything would look better in the morning," he finished.

We're history! We are so busted! If there were even an inch of sand in front of him, Tom would gladly have buried his head in it. Although that wasn't necessary because Todd had just buried them both.

Tom closed his eyes.

"Just what the heck is going on here!" Elizabeth's voice rose in anger. "I thought Jessica found her purse!"

"Tension, this is good!" Tom heard Ned whisper as the cameramen zoomed in. There was no way out.

"You guys are lying about something." Elizabeth swung around to face Tom. "Tell me, Tom, did

81

you really think that after all the investigative reporting I've done, I wouldn't figure out that you were lying?" she said sarcastically.

"Look, can we talk about this in private?" Tom whispered, trying for Elizabeth's sake to sound calm and reasonable, but Elizabeth waved him off as if he were an insect.

"A private conference isn't going to help you here. Just tell me—tell us all!—where my sister is and whatever else it is you're trying to cover up!" Elizabeth's cheeks were flushed dark red with anger, and she folded her shaking arms. "I'm waiting," she added harshly. "And I want the truth this time!"

A cameraman pointed his lens at Tom. It made him feel as if he were staring down the barrel of a gun. There was nowhere to hide. And judging by the look on Elizabeth's face, Tom would have every reason to hide once she knew the full story.

Tom shot Todd an icy look before he spoke. "Jessica's not here," he said. "Elizabeth, I was trying to protect you from the truth, but Todd couldn't keep his big mouth shut."

"Give it up, Watts! What are you, the big rescuer?" Todd yelled.

"Shut up!" Elizabeth shouted. "Tone down the testosterone," she continued coldly, "because I'm not interested in either of you. Now, I'm going to ask you again and for the last time: Where is my sister?"

"That's a good question," Tom replied grimly. "She could be anywhere by now." *And boy, do I wish I were her,* he thought as misery and helplessness threatened to swallow him whole. *I'd give a million bucks to be anywhere but here!*

Jessica, you are one tough cookie! Jessica sighed happily and slurped on her super-sized diet Coke, reflecting on the past couple of days and congratulating herself for handling trauma so well.

Since her unfortunate sighting of Team One, she'd somehow managed to pick up the pieces and move on. Of course, Elvis had certainly helped, soothing her with calming words and, most important, demonstrating that he was a man of action, unafraid to step on the accelerator and take her away from it all, leaving RVs and their back-stabbing passengers far, far behind.

Jessica gloated as she reflected on the devastation she'd left in her wake. Pure carnage! *They won't forget me in a hurry ever again!* she smirked, reliving each genius insult she'd hurled, each perfect put-down, right down to the final hair-tossing exit. And in a Cadillac, no less! No one could deny it. Drama—Jessica Wakefield style—was utterly glamorous!

"What're you dreaming about, little lady?"

"Memphis." Jessica glanced coyly at Elvis, smoothly guiding the car to Memphis with its promise of nonstop, all-night fun. The perfect place to lose yourself—and find yourself, as Elvis liked to put it. And Jessica was ready to do just that and more. Especially with a studly sophisticate, the kind of man well mannered enough to pay for her to have her own room at night, a man who treated her with the respect she deserved.

Her new adventure wasn't all a bed of roses. More like a bed of fleas! Jessica wrinkled her sun-peeled nose at the thought of the ghastly little motel they'd stayed at last night. But there'd hardly been much of a choice, and she was sure if there'd been a Four Seasons Hotel nearby, Elvis would have been only too happy to foot the bill. Such a gentleman! A dreamy smile played across the corners of Jessica's lips even as she pondered the downside to all this impeccable southern grace. It could get a tad bit dull if left unchecked. But she wasn't worried. If Elvis had so far behaved a bit too impeccably for Jessica's liking, well, they had all the time in the world to work on that.

"Check out that rock formation over there! Looks like it's been chiseled." Elvis pointed out yet another natural landmark, and Jessica stifled a yawn. Though she loved driving in the open air, she still found the landscape itself profoundly dreary. She smiled contentedly as her eyes lingered on the only chiseled formation that interested her—Elvis's strong jawline.

"Tell me if you get tired of driving," Jessica purred seductively. "We could always take a quick rest stop and I could give you my famous neck rub," she added mischievously.

"I'd like that," Elvis said.

Score one for Miss Monroe! Jessica batted her lashes at Elvis and congratulated herself when he shot her a steamy, come-hither smile. Flirting truly was an effortless art. You were either born with the talent or doomed to a life of lonely Saturday nights. *Luckily I know exactly how to read a man,* Jessica thought contentedly. Suddenly she froze midsmile as an image of Neil contradicted her happy moment.

Jessica felt her face flush scarlet as she pictured Neil preparing for whatever event he'd have to get through the next day. *He's probably thanking the gods that I'm finally out of his hair,* she thought, frowning.

"Aw, shucks, honey. Something bothering you?" Elvis queried gently as tears welled up in Jessica's eyes.

Jessica sniffed. "Nothing. Just wondering what the team's doing without me. And if I did the right thing," she added with a whimper. Maybe she had been too quick to run away. And she certainly couldn't keep running forever.

"Well, just you remember, I'm at your service," Elvis offered kindly as Jessica felt a tide of tears spilling onto her cheeks. "And if you want to go back, I'll take you."

"But I don't even know where they are now!"

Jessica wailed. "And who are we trying to kid? They won't want me back!"

Elvis pulled over to the shoulder of the road, and Jessica threw herself into his arms, convulsing in anguish. It was all very well trying to tell herself she was justified in splitting, but what if she'd just made a major mistake she could never undo?

"Listen here," Elvis said calmly as he stroked Jessica's hair. "This thing seems bigger than it really is. Just remember, it's only a game. Just a silly road-trip competition. One day you'll look back on this little bend in that road and laugh."

"You really think so?" Jessica said hesitantly through her tears.

"I know so. Believe me, darlin', I've seen these kinds of tiffs all through my musical career. It's nothin' more than a storm in a teacup. And if you really want to go back to your team, then we'll call up that TV station and ask them where you need to be and when."

As Jessica snuggled into Elvis's chest, she began to feel calmer. She could get back to the team if she needed to. It would be tricky but not impossible—and they were in the lead anyway, so her having gone AWOL for a while probably hadn't hurt them. Jessica relaxed and concentrated on the feel of Elvis's sculpted biceps through his thin silk shirt. Now that she knew there was a way she could track the team down, she suddenly felt a lot less pressured to charge back with her tail between her legs—particularly when there were other, much more tantalizing possibilities ahead.

"So, what'll it be? Shall we keep going?" Elvis prompted gently.

Jessica sat up and wiped her eyes. "You bet!" she retorted. "Memphis, it is. And pronto, please. I've had just about all the wide-open space I can take!"

Maybe she would decide to rejoin the competition at a later stage, but as Elvis screeched back onto the asphalt, Jessica seriously doubted she ever would. The tacky, tortoiselike Winnebago was hardly her sort of vehicle, and the Coast-to-Coast gang were simply not her kind of people. Frankly, Jessica was beginning to wonder why she even cared what they thought of her or what they were up to. *Probably something only marginally less embarrassing than potato-sack or egg-and-spoon races!* she thought with a smirk.

Maybe they were all better off cutting their losses. Watching the Caddy's speedometer leap from eighty to a hundred in a nanosecond, Jessica knew that she certainly was. No question about it: This life was definitely more her speed!

Chapter Six

"We're coming at you live from Clover Park, St. Joseph, Missouri, and this is event number four! Welcome, Coast-to-Coasters, and welcome to all you audience members at home!" cried Richie Valentine, ICSN's host and one of the most popular TV sports personalities on cable TV.

"As you can see, our hot and sweaty tribe of teen teamsters have been hoofing it up on horseback." Richie waved expansively at the teams, some of whom were still on their horses, others lolling exhaustedly on a grassy bank. "Yes, they've been hitting the dirt, and boy, does it hurt, am I right, guys? Nudge, nudge, wink, wink, if ya know what I mean! Heh heh!"

Someone save us all! Elizabeth rolled her eyes as Richie blabbered on. Perhaps she was only imagining things, but it seemed that with each successive event, Richie had become more and more annoyingly peppy and ridiculous. *Or maybe I've just lost my sense of humor,* Elizabeth considered grimly. Not exactly a stretch when she considered the past five hours.

Event four was, in Elizabeth's opinion, by far the most grueling of all the events. As part of the preevent activities, they'd had to ride around on horseback, reenacting the old Pony Express with pretend mailbags, making mail drops around the town. That in itself wouldn't have been so bad if it weren't for the stiff, heavy, nineteenth-century costumes they had to sweat through as the merciless sun beat down on them all day. To make matters worse, Elizabeth had had the bad fortune of being partnered with Sam. She'd spent almost the entire day riding around with a person who, when he wasn't pretending she didn't even exist, was calling her "chick" or "blondie."

Like I need the extra stress! Elizabeth fumed, tasting dirt under her tongue. And while Richie blathered on, explaining Team One's automatic disqualification "as a result of Jessica Wakefield's mysterious disappearance," Elizabeth felt a knot of tension the size of a grapefruit swell inside her stomach. It was not a day worth remembering. And it wasn't over yet.

"And now for the event itself! Teams, folks at home, this is going to be one wild race, I'll tell you that!" *Yeah, then tell us already,* Elizabeth thought impatiently, gingerly rearranging herself on the grass. Every bone ached, and every muscle screamed for mercy.

"The culmination of a hard day's work begins when I wave the ICSN red flag, at which point our teams here will commence with a mailbag relay race. Each participant must pass the bag to their teammates, who will be stationed at the various marked flag points throughout the park. Whoever makes it home first wins, and a dropped mailbag means disqualification. Teams, find your positions and get ready. In five minutes the relay will commence!"

OK, here goes! Elizabeth walked over to the hitching post, swung a leg over her horse, a feisty chestnut Arab, and cantered over to what she was told was her starting position: fourth, at a post on a sloping lawn. As the rest of the teams made their way to the designated "mail-drop" stops, Elizabeth felt her heart begin to beat louder with anticipation. And when she heard a distant "Yeehaw!" and a thunder of hooves, she hunched forward in her saddle. Through the bushes she could see bobbing heads and riders. And Charlie, cleanly making the first drop straight into Ruby's hands.

"Go, Ruby!" Elizabeth shouted excitedly as she spotted Ruby's head of dark curls bouncing above the bushes. Ruby made the drop into Uli's hands just as Team Three's Cynthia Lewis dropped a bag. But something was slowing Uli down. Team Four was well ahead, already dropping at position four. "C'mon, Uli! You're almost there!"

"Got it!" Elizabeth shouted, cracking the reins as Uli tossed the mailbag into her hand at last. She dug her heels into her horse's sides and fixed her eyes ahead, feeling the thundery thrill of the horse beneath her, a surge of excitement combining with the adrenaline coursing through her veins. They were going to win!

Out of the corner of her eye Elizabeth spotted Team Four's speedy Mickey James overtaking her—and felt her confidence drop away. Mickey was faster than anybody on any team, whether on his own two legs or on a horse. Worse, she could see Sam standing up impatiently in his stirrups, evidently disappointed as Mickey successfully made his drop before Elizabeth. *He doesn't think I can ride!* Elizabeth thought angrily, snapping at the reins and digging her heels into the Arab's flanks. But no matter how much she urged the horse on, Sam was still far away, maybe too far if she kept to the path. If . . .

Scanning quickly sideways, Elizabeth spotted a fence. If she cleared it, she would have a straight path to Sam, and the shortcut would place them back in the running for the lead. If!

Elizabeth had only a split second to make her decision. She could either go for it and keep the team in the running or take the safe path and come in second.

Better safe than sorry! Elizabeth thought, instinctively recoiling from the risk. *Nothing ventured, nothing gained!* another part of her snapped in response. Elizabeth felt her heart begin to quicken, and for once the risky option seemed the right one. Maybe it was time to ignore the cautious voice that had led her for so long.

This is my chance! Elizabeth told herself, sharply yanking on the reins to make the horse veer left. She had a point to prove—to Sam and to herself.

Elizabeth neared the fence, urged the horse on, and leaned forward. *I can do this!* she told herself, a bolt of confidence burning like an electric current through her veins. And in that moment Elizabeth felt more alive than she ever had in her whole life.

Focus! Elizabeth concentrated on the other side of the fence and on Sam in the distance. *Lean forward, let the horse know you're in charge . . . now!*

Suddenly she felt as if someone had poked a knitting needle through her ribs. Terror sliced and ripped through her body as her instincts sounded the piercing alarm: There was no way she could hack it! She'd totally misjudged the height of the fence!

The fence rose up in a flash of metal as Elizabeth's inner voice offered its own cruelly useless message: *I told you so!* But it was too late to back out. There was nowhere to go but forward. *Help!* The word died before it could even escape her lips.

*　　　*　　　*

"Elizabeth!" Sam yelled, his voice coming out in a hoarse croak as he galloped toward her. One moment she was there on the path, riding smoothly, perfectly in control. The next thing she'd suddenly and without any warning turned sharply and steered the horse toward a suicide obstacle. Out of her mind! Sam had thought, disbelieving, until he realized she really meant to attempt to clear the fence.

Only a crazy daredevil would even try to pull a wacko move like that. Elizabeth was a lot of things, but she was definitely not the wild, stunt-chick type. Still, she had jumped out of their white-water raft to save Ruby. . . . Sam swallowed hard. What he was seeing was all too frighteningly real.

Rigid with fear, he sped toward Elizabeth even though he knew he was too late to stop her. He could only watch helplessly as she rose up into the air, her blond hair whipping around her face as the horse shot upward, jerking its head to the side.

"It's Wakefield!" Sam heard a cameraman shout, but the voice sounded very far away. He heard other yells too, the panic as people realized what was about to happen, but it was as if he were underwater or imprisoned in a glass box. All Sam could see was Elizabeth, her hand letting the reins slip, her body folding forward—all in one awful, long, slow-motion second that seemed eternal.

Please make it! Sam begged silently as his heart

beat with a dull, sickening thud in time to the pounding of his horse's hooves.

"She's going to break her neck!" Sam heard someone shout. He watched Elizabeth's head snap back as her body lurched out of the saddle.

"Just hold on!" Sam yelled. "You're going to be OK!" But Elizabeth had as much control over her situation as a paper airplane in a tornado. And everything was dangerously, fatally wrong. Her feet were out of the stirrups now, her body crumpling over.

Elizabeth uttered a strangled sob, and Sam felt the sound go right through him. *You've got to save her!* he thought wildly, although he knew there was absolutely nothing he could do. She was going to fall, and Sam knew there was no way she'd make it through the accident unharmed.

"Noooo!" Elizabeth screamed as she felt herself slipping down toward the horse's neck, the reins flying out of her grasp.

"Just hold on!" she heard Sam scream, but she had nothing to hold on to. All she had was the mailbag, held in an iron grip of terror in one hand as her other hand scratched at the air.

Use your legs! Suddenly Elizabeth thought of her junior-high-school riding coach and concentrated all her energy on forcing her thighs to grip the horse's sides. Her muscles burned and tore with strain. Almost there . . .

After what seemed an eternity, the horse's front hooves slammed into the grass as he landed clear, but Elizabeth's entire body was sliding down now, over the left of the horse's heaving body.

She saw the ground whip past her in a fast-motion blend of green and brown. She clawed at the horse's neck with her free hand, grabbing for a fistful of dark, matted mane. Yes! She clung to the mane with every ounce of strength she possessed. It was her only chance for survival. If she fell off, she knew she'd break her back or get crushed under the horse's back hooves.

Bam! The back hooves came down and Elizabeth bounced upright again. And then Sam was in front of her, a shooting arrow, dirt flying up from all angles as he raced toward her on his horse.

The bag! Elizabeth thought woodenly, trying to relax the viselike grip of her hand and extending her arm to the side. It was almost as if the shock had turned her into a robot. Just a little longer . . . She had to hang on! She'd come this far.

Sam was almost there, almost at her side, but Elizabeth felt as if he were a mile away. Her body had begun to register the shock of her near miss, and she felt as limp as a blob of Jell-O, her muscles weakening, melting into nothing. A few more seconds . . . She held out her hand, but her grip was slipping, her hand clammy with perspiration.

I'm going to drop it, Elizabeth thought numbly.

Sam was close. She needed just a second more, but it was a second that came a second too late.

She let go.

"Got it!" Sam yelled triumphantly as a distant crowd cheered. But the only sound Elizabeth could fully register was that of her thundering heart, slamming at her rib cage and booming through her eardrums. She was still alive.

"Liz!" Tom yelled over the pounding of his horse's hooves. "I'm coming!" Of course, the horse wasn't really his to ride since Team One had been blocked from competing in the event altogether. But that hadn't stopped Tom. One look at Elizabeth in distress and he'd grabbed the nearest horse he could find and pounded straight after her, his mouth dry with fear, his instinct to protect her sharper than it had ever been since he'd known her.

What was she thinking? Tom had seen it all happen, following Elizabeth's progress with his binoculars, watching her sudden swerve and heart-stopping jump with terrified amazement. Just one look at the horse shying away from the fence and Tom could see that Elizabeth was in serious trouble.

Still, it was inconceivable to him that she could have pulled such a lunatic move just to help her team win. Jessica, maybe, but Elizabeth would never do something so downright crazy. *At least not the Liz I know* . . . But there was no time to reflect on that now. Elizabeth needed him, and he needed to be there.

"Liz! I'm right here!" Tom practically dismounted in midair and rushed over to where Elizabeth sat on the grass, surrounded by anxious bystanders, park wardens, the quivering, sweat-lathered horse, and ICSN crew members. Elizabeth's head was on her arms, her skin flushed with fright.

"Coming through!" Tom announced impatiently, pushing to get to Elizabeth. All of a sudden applause broke out, and Tom followed the collective gaze to spot Team Two's Josh Margolin crossing the finish line to win the race. As the group congratulated Elizabeth on her save, Tom felt a sharp elbow in his ribs as someone struggled to get to Elizabeth first. Sam Burgess.

Tom's jaw stiffened in anger. He liked Burgess even less than he liked Wilkins. The guy thought he was just too cool for his own good, a real heartbreaker with his scruffy, slacker look and offhand attitude to anyone who wore a belt and had some ambition in life. A total light-weight!

Usually Tom wouldn't be so bothered by someone like Sam, but he didn't like the way Sam acted around Elizabeth—any more than he liked the way Elizabeth acted around Sam. His presence seemed to make her hyperaware of herself, awkward somehow. He'd heard about that kiss on the

dance floor too—how first Sam had run Todd off.
. . . *Right now Burgess shouldn't be around at all!*
Tom fumed. Sam was half the problem in the first
place. Sure, Elizabeth's team had won the race,
but if Sam were a real man, if he really cared about
her, he'd never have let Elizabeth pull that stunt
without risking his neck to save her! And now it
was just a little too late to trot back after the fact
and hope everything was hunky-dory.

"Uh, Sam, why don't you take a chill pill for a
moment, all right, pal? I can take it from here,"
said Tom tersely, pushing past him toward
Elizabeth. "Are you OK, Liz?" he asked anxiously,
kneeling down to place a concerned hand on her
shoulder as Sam shrugged and turned away. That
had been easy! Tom felt manly and in control and
hoped Elizabeth would see him that way. He was
ready to do anything for her, anything to prove he
could take care of her. Maybe then she'd forgive
him for not taking care of Jessica. . . .

"Do you need something? Ice water?" Tom
asked gently.

"I'm fine," Elizabeth replied coolly, her eyes
fixed to the left of Tom's head, watching Sam walk
away. "Sam, don't go!" she called weakly. "Tell me
the score."

"Uh—sure!" Sam raised an eyebrow at Tom
and made his way back to Elizabeth. Slighted,
Tom had no choice but to back away. *Apparently
the score is zero for Watts!* he thought grimly. If

only he'd been allowed to compete, he could have rescued Elizabeth and regained her respect. Instead he'd had to stand on the sidelines, exactly where he was now.

But not for long, Tom promised himself, scowling as he watched Sam cozying up to Elizabeth. The trip was only half over, and although Tom had lost some points with Elizabeth, he wasn't about to give up. Just one strategic move could tip the scales in his favor. Nothing was final yet.

Chapter Seven

"Thanks," Elizabeth murmured as Sam brought her a cup of water.

"It has sugar in it—for shock."

"Maybe you could use a little of this yourself," Elizabeth joked, noting the ashy color of Sam's usually golden-tanned face. Obviously her near miss had really shaken him up. *And maybe that means he really does care for me!* she thought.

If not, he'd put on a great act, rushing over to see what she needed. And when she'd tried to get up to walk over to a park bench, he'd caught her as she stumbled, weakened by muscle strain. Then without a word he'd lifted her in his strong arms and carried her across the lawn. At first Elizabeth had tried to protest. She didn't want to draw any more attention to herself than she already had, but she felt too shaky to walk, and her **head** was still reeling. And wrapped in Sam's arms, Elizabeth felt safe and protected, although the proximity of his strong chest only made her palpitating heart skip even faster.

"Yeah, I'll take a sip of your water." Sam smiled weakly, shaking his dirt- and sun-streaked hair out of his eyes. "That was some move you pulled, Wakefield," he added, his fingers grazing hers as he took the paper cup from her hand.

"Just trying to score some points," Elizabeth replied, averting her eyes from Sam's piercing gaze.

"You don't have to kill yourself to get my attention," Sam retorted with an enigmatic smile.

"Excuse me?" Elizabeth's cheeks suddenly blazed in anger. "Someone around here is delusional," she added icily.

"And someone's in denial," Sam countered evenly. Was that a smirk? Elizabeth felt as if someone had just dumped a tray of ice cubes down the back of her shirt. What was Sam's problem? One moment he seemed open and genuinely caring, and then with a sudden shift he transformed into an arrogant jerk.

"I don't have to listen to this," Elizabeth began hotly, shooting to her feet. "I—"

"Shhh." Sam pulled her back down, silencing her with a finger to her lips. "Relax. You're still weak," he murmured, leaning in closer, his finger gently tracing the line of her lower lip.

"I won't deny that. . . ." Elizabeth closed her

102

eyes. Although a part of her was indignantly kicking and screaming, that part was drowned out by the fiery sensation spreading from her lips down to her neck. *I'm definitely losing it!* she thought. Too late. Elizabeth knew she was already gone, her lips parting as she waited for Sam's soft yet demanding lips to close onto her own.

"Uh, I think that's the score! I'm gonna go check it out."

Startled, Elizabeth's eyelids flew open. "You already told me the score!"

"Yeah, for this event. But they're announcing the cumulative scores now," Sam replied, pulling away and hooking his thumbs into his belt loops. Suddenly his eyes were blank, fixed on the crowd beyond the trees. "You'll be OK," he added impersonally. "Tom and Company will be only too pleased to come and get you," he added, turning away.

"Come and get me?" Elizabeth repeated incredulously. "What am I? A stray dog?" But Sam was already striding purposefully away, his back to her. *A ball and chain around your ankle, is that what I am?* Elizabeth felt like screaming out, but she only bit her lip and narrowed her eyes bitterly. She didn't need to ask Sam anything. She knew the answer to her own question. She was just a pawn in Sam's nasty little game. And once again he'd knocked her right off the chessboard. *But for the last time,* Elizabeth vowed. *Game over!*

*   *   *

"And the scores as they now stand: Team One still leads with 110 points despite the disappearance of player Jessica Wakefield; Teams Two and Four, in close second with 100 points. Then we have Team Three bringing up the rear at fifty!" Richie boomed, his moon face filling the diner's small TV screen.

"Jessica! They mentioned you again! Golly, y'all, a real, live celebrity in our little diner!" screeched Laverne, a menthol cigarette in the corner of her mouth wagging with each word, her thickly frosted eyelids opening wide in wonder.

"Now, now, Laverne," Jessica replied demurely, fanning away both mentholated smoke and the waitress's compliment with a sweep of her hand. But she couldn't deny the thrill tingling at her spine as she drank in the palpable admiration oozing from the very walls of Pop's Palace. Even with all its difficulties, Jessica had to admit that running away was very chic.

And Laverne wasn't exactly far from the truth. Fame, like anything else, was relative, and as Jessica cast her eyes around the Memphis diner with its charming but homely crew of regulars, she saw things through the eyes of the simple, common folk and had to concur.

"You're like Amelia Earhart, missy," an elderly, toothless gentleman added, pointing a bony finger toward the TV screen. "You're all they talk about. Everybody wants to know where you are."

"Yup, you're the star, kiddo," Elvis added, winking at Jessica.

Toying with a forkful of cherry pie, Jessica couldn't deny the truth, although she really didn't want to make a fuss. All this talk about her was rather embarrassing in its way, but judging from the TV broadcast, she realized that her disappearance was indeed something of a national crisis, probably being discussed in homes across America that very minute.

And with that kind of fame came a lot of responsibility! Jessica sighed, blanching as she thought of Elizabeth's narrow brush with disaster. Clearly Elizabeth was so distraught over Jessica's absence, it had driven her clean out of her mind, transforming her from a predictable tortoise into a turbopowered hare.

Luckily everything had turned out to be OK with Elizabeth, but for a second there Jessica's heart had been in her mouth. Seeing poor Elizabeth shaking with shock was a real wake-up call. *I've really caused a major wig-out fest!* Jessica fretted. It was screamingly obvious that her disappearance was causing her twin sister real psychological trauma, even forcing her to try to become Jessica by pulling the sort of maneuver Jessica pulled all the time. A stunt that practically rocked Elizabeth right out of the world of the living! Jessica bit her lip and stared pensively into her coffee. What had she done? And was it too late to put things right?

105

"Don't drop your lip. You need your down-time, hon," Laverne offered sympathetically, exhaling a stream of smoke. "It's gotta be exhausting surrounded by all that paparazzi and glamour day in, day out. I don't blame you for cuttin' and runnin'."

"It's tough at the top!" Pearl, another waitress, agreed, her white lacquered beehive quivering as she nodded vigorously. "I think being a star is a very difficult calling," she added, squeezing Jessica's shoulder, her long mauve talons digging into Jessica's flesh.

"It's certainly not easy," Jessica trilled, beaming as Laverne handed her another generous helping of cherry pie. As she tucked into the rich dessert, a wave of benevolence swept over her. These were good, wholesome people, tacky in the taste department, but bighearted. And it was nice to have their support and goodwill during this difficult time. *Perhaps I should autograph this pie plate!* Jessica wondered, scraping cream from the plain blue-and-white crockery. *Just a small gesture from me, just one insignificant little moment of my time that will affect the rest of their lives . . .*

"Elizabeth, any special message for your sister?" Richie Valentine intoned, breaking into Jessica's reverie.

Jessica drew breath sharply as Elizabeth's worried face filled the screen. "I just want to know that she's OK. That's all that counts. Please, Jess, if you're listening, let us know where you are."

Liz! Jessica felt tears spring to her eyes as she saw her sister's pale face. *I've got to let her know I'm all right!*

"Oh, my Lord, I'm going to cry!" Laverne squawked, the cigarette trembling with emotion. "Honey, what are you going to do?"

"Our next event stop—the one and only Chicago!" Richie continued as the diner fell into reverent silence and Jessica considered her options.

Finally Jessica spoke. "First, I'm going to get on the phone and call my sister. And then, well, it looks like I'm going to have to go. I'd love to have stayed," she added, smiling bravely at Elvis. "You and I—we could have painted this town red." Jessica lowered her head dramatically and paused before looking up. "But it was not meant to be. Duty calls, and I must face the music. 'Cause I've been running too long."

Bummer, Jessica thought miserably, her eyes traveling the length of Elvis's broad chest. He had one heck of a body, and she was sorry to miss out. Unfortunately things seemed to go a little slower with these southern types, and Jessica was pretty much out of time.

"Bravo!" Pearl clapped, and the others slowly joined in.

"Whatever you say, little lady," Elvis replied, touching Jessica's cheek. "Chicago needs you. But you can wait until tomorrow, can't you?"

107

"Wanna paint the town red?" Jessica grinned and swiveled on her bar stool. "The night is young."

"You're right about that last part." Elvis curled his lip in a sexy smile and leaned forward, catching Jessica's bar stool midspin. "But as for a night on the town, well, I had something else in mind," he whispered huskily. "Something a little quieter. How about coming over to my place?"

"Your place?" Jessica breathed as Elvis's stubbly cheek grazed her ear.

"It's a pretty nice pad, if I do say so myself. Kind of wild. I think you'll like it."

So do I, Jessica thought dreamily as she felt Elvis's hot breath on her neck. "So, how about it, Marilyn?"

Wild . . . Jessica lowered her lashes and moistened her lips. Things were definitely starting to heat up. And not a minute too soon! With an expert toss of her thick, blond mane Jessica leaned toward Elvis and placed her hands around his neck, a wicked smile playing at the corners of her lips. "Darlin'," she whispered back, twanging seductively in his ear, "I thought you'd never ask!"

"Sam, that was one heck of a save you made." Ned thrust the microphone in front of Sam's face with one hand and slapped him on the back with the other. "Tell us how it felt!"

A lot better than I feel right now, Sam thought

grimly as he muttered a monosyllabic answer for Ned's dorky, behind-the-scenes docudrama. Right then all Sam wanted to do was pack up his army bag, hit the dust, and hitchhike his way out of what was becoming a way more stressful situation than he'd bargained for—especially in the Elizabeth Wakefield department.

As if on cue, Elizabeth walked right past, her face impassive, her eyes firmly avoiding Sam's. *And that's fine with me!* Sam thought angrily, kicking at a small stone. He knew he was being ridiculous, hypocritical even, but Elizabeth also had her part to play in their latest argument, over-reacting to everything he'd said to her back at the park bench. And it wasn't like he hadn't bent over backward to make sure she was OK, carrying her away from the crowd and bringing her sugared water. What more could he have done?

Of course, there'd been a wobbly moment when Sam knew he was playing with fire, almost kissing Elizabeth, almost starting the whole thing up again. But that was understandable, consider-ing the emotional overdrive they'd been thrown into by Elizabeth's close call. *But that's over now,* Sam thought, dismissing from his mind the horri-ble memory of Elizabeth hanging off the leaping horse. No matter how tempting, kissing Elizabeth wouldn't have solved anything. He'd realized that almost immediately after he'd left her alone on the dance floor. Sam knew he couldn't live up to

Elizabeth's expectations. If only she would realize that, see that he was doing them both a favor.

Yeah, right! Sam closed his eyes, willing the image to go away, but it wouldn't: Elizabeth's perfect, high-cheekboned face, her soft, bow-shaped mouth waiting for his kiss. Who would be crazy enough to turn down that kind of opportunity? Only an extreme loser . . .

"Sam, you're the man, buddy!" Josh interrupted Sam's gloomy thoughts with a loud whoop. "We won, dude! Whoo-hoo!"

"You sure kicked the buttock out there!" Uli agreed, and Sam had to laugh, feeling his spirits lighten as the guys and some members of the other teams came by to offer congratulations.

Suddenly Sam didn't feel like such a loser. Sure, Elizabeth probably thought he was scum, but then she'd thought that ever since she met him. *And I can't do squat about that now!* Sam rationalized as Josh tossed him a beer. Now was neither the time nor the place for the groveling Elizabeth would require from him. Plus she needed to cool down first before he could approach her—and that could take days. *Drink now, deal later!* Sam thought as Uli hoisted him onto his shoulders. And why not? He'd lost Elizabeth's respect, but not everyone hated him. Right now he was a big shot, the man who made the save. And that was something—wasn't it?

* * *

"Graceland!" Jessica squealed with laughter as the Caddy purred to a standstill outside the giant gates. "Oh, Elvis, you kill me, you really do."

"As promised, my humble abode, ma'am," Elvis explained with a chuckle, leaping out of the car.

"Pity we can't get in," Jessica murmured, staring beyond the iron gates at the mansion. She couldn't see much more than lots of tiny lights, glittering in the darkness.

"What do you mean? What man can't get into his own house?" Elvis responded, pulling Jessica out of the car impatiently. "I just choose a more unconventional route," he added. "C'mon, I'll show you!"

"This is total lunacy," Jessica whispered, stifling a giggle as Elvis hoisted her into a giant tree growing through a part of the wrought-iron fence.

"Right behind you, admiring the view," Elvis replied saucily, and Jessica swatted him with a kick of her left mule. "Now slide onto the lower branch. . . ."

"Yikes!" Jessica wailed as she crashed onto the lawn, a sharp twig clawing her on her way down. But nothing was harmed. Nothing a few kisses wouldn't fix anyway.

"Just a little farther." Elvis led Jessica by the hand up a small, sloping hill and down the other side. "There!"

"Well, I'll be—"

"Priscilla Beaulieu Presley? Just for a night?"

111

Elvis gestured toward the scene before them. "Care to partake of our private swimming pool, honey?"

"It's—incredible!" Jessica breathed, unable to take her eyes off the shimmering, electric blue, oval pool in front of her. Lit by sunken underwater lights, the pool looked as if it were studded with a million twinkling rhinestones. Jessica clapped in delight and then shot Elvis a look of alarm.

"Oh, don't worry," Elvis reassured her, lazily unbuttoning his shirt and slipping out of his blue suede shoes. "I've sent the servants home," he added grandly. "Really, don't worry, Priscilla. We'll keep an eye out for security."

"Sounds fantastic!" Jessica purred as she slipped out of her platforms.

"Don't you want to take off more than that?" Elvis teased, walking lazily toward Jessica.

"Slow down, pal!" Jessica threw back her head and laughed. From zero to a hundred in a matter of seconds! The guy was as good as his car! "I think I can swim in this," she added with a grin, sliding her hands down her skimpy, formfitting black Lycra dress. "It's like a second skin."

They walked to the edge of the glittering pool. With a light spring Jessica arced her body up into the air and executed a perfect swan dive.

Within a fraction of a second Elvis was by her side, enjoying the deliciously cool water. "Speaking of skin," Elvis murmured, gently encircling Jessica's lower back with his strong hands and pulling her into lower water where they could stand. "I've been noticing how flawless yours is, Priscilla."

"And there I was thinking you saw me as just a poor little girl you felt obligated to rescue." Jessica pouted as she slid her hands up Elvis's taut arms to his glistening shoulders.

"Just waiting for the right moment—and I think this is it." Elvis gently massaged Jessica's lower back as his lips nuzzled her neck.

"Mmmm, I think you're right," she murmured. Jessica felt Elvis's mouth nibbling her chin, moving up toward her waiting lips. She closed her eyes, shivering with blissful anticipation. And as Elvis's lips grazed her own, his mouth urgent but gentle, his hands tracing small circles across her back, she felt as if she were drowning in pleasure.

"Wow," Jessica whispered when they finally came up for air. "Careful, I might drown," she warned jokingly.

"In that case," Elvis said, kissing her on the nose, "I'll have to take you into the jungle room for mouth-to-mouth resuscitation."

Jessica snuggled into Elvis's chest with a satisfied smile. It was a pity she had to leave for Chicago in the morning, but despite all the nastiness that might lie ahead, she knew she would never regret this amazing detour. This was living! After all, how many people got to experience Elvis Presley's famed magnetism firsthand?

Chapter
Eight

Four down, four to go! Elizabeth shifted gears, easing the Winnebago down the interstate. She felt surprisingly good, considering her experience with the competition so far. The day before she'd have given her right arm to pack up and ditch the competition, but today, Saturday, she felt kind of antsy to get to Illinois and curious about what lay in store for them there.

Maybe I'm just glad to be alive! Elizabeth reflected, smiling at Charlie, riding shotgun next to her. She slid a dance music tape into the cassette player, and the strains of "I'm Every Woman" began to pump through the speakers. Elizabeth nodded to the beat. Right at that moment, with the breeze coming in through the open window and tickling her hair, Elizabeth felt lighter and more even keeled than she had in a long time.

Even Sam and Jessica, the two deadweights on Elizabeth's shoulders, seem to have been spirited away. Especially Sam. *His problems are his, not mine!* she reminded herself. And for the first time she didn't really care whether his behavior was passive-aggressive or just downright aggressive. Either way, Sam would have to sort himself out without her.

I am every woman! Elizabeth thought, lifting her chin defiantly. And she wasn't going to apologize for it! If Sam couldn't meet the challenge, he was free to go—to Florida if that's what he wanted! Elizabeth stepped on the accelerator, feeling powerful and self-controlled. Sam and his yo-yoing mood swings would no longer be tolerated. *I'm in the driver's seat now—in every way!*

"Uh, Liz, can you pull over?" Charlie said just as Elizabeth was about to belt out the chorus of her new theme song. "I think I'm going to be sick!" Charlie added weakly.

Elizabeth took one look at Charlie, her usually rosy cheeks tinged a sickly green, and screeched to a halt on the side of the highway.

Charlie practically fell out of the Winnebago and pelted down the embankment. Elizabeth jumped out after her. "Charlie, are you OK?" she called out anxiously as Charlie retched dryly.

"I'm fine," Charlie murmured as Elizabeth rushed to her friend's side with a bottle of spring water. "Just carsick—you know me," she joked feebly, gratefully accepting the water. "I'll be OK in a sec," she added, but Elizabeth wasn't so sure. Charlie's face was practically the color of the gray

Indian cotton dress she had on, and there were dark, bruise-colored circles under her eyes.

Elizabeth looked searchingly into Charlie's eyes, concerned that she hadn't paid more attention to her friend over the past few days. Because she wasn't just carsick—that much was obvious.

"Charlie," Elizabeth prodded gently, "what's really wrong? Tell me, please. Because you haven't been yourself lately."

"Honestly, it's nothing, Liz," Charlie protested as she started back toward the Winnebago. "I'll be fine when we get to Peoria," she added over her shoulder. "I guess I'm just really excited about seeing Scott again, and I'm not used to all this driving. . . ."

Could that be all it was? Elizabeth wondered as she slowly got back into the driver's seat. She cast a wary eye at Charlie. Although she wanted to, Elizabeth wasn't buying the girl's explanation. Charlie didn't look like someone thrilled at the prospect of seeing her boyfriend after several days' absence. And she didn't look like someone with a minor case of stomach trouble either.

She's hiding something, Elizabeth concluded, her heart constricting as she glanced at the pale girl in the seat beside her. Elizabeth knew Charlie wasn't about to confess her troubles, at least not just now. But as she slid the key into the ignition, Elizabeth vowed she would get the truth out of Charlie eventually.

Because something definitely wasn't right, and

Elizabeth couldn't watch her friend suffer in silence for much longer.

"Give it a rest, would you?" Neil yelled, shaking his head as he listened to Todd and Tom bickering like five-year-olds in the backseat. "Worse than Felix and Oscar," he added wryly to Rob, riding shotgun next to him. "Someone should syndicate that mutual loathing. There could be big money in it."

Rob nodded and squeezed his temples as Neil pumped the gas mercilessly. Every moment on the road was sheer torture with the endless "who-said-what-to-Elizabeth-Wakefield" sound track running behind them, and all Neil wanted was to get to Peoria without developing a tumor. *One Wakefield's enough trouble!* he mused darkly. It was almost comical how much emotional venting the twins had managed to inspire, Elizabeth as the object of Tom and Todd's collective worship and Jessica . . . Well, Neil didn't even want to go there. It was pointless reflecting on things beyond his control.

"Cut it out, will you?" Rob snarled, twisting his head around to glare at Wilkins and Watts. "It's useless!" He sighed and rolled his bloodshot eyes at Neil. "They're obsessed!"

And they're not the only ones! Neil gritted his teeth, steeling himself for the inevitable whine to come.

"Robbie-pookie-boy!" Right on cue! "Boo-boo," Pam squealed nasally from the back, "pay me some attention. I'm looonely!"

"Rob, will you tell her to pipe down? That girl of yours is adding seriously to the carcinogenic vibe in here," Neil muttered irritably. Rob nodded glumly but remained mute in the face of his overpowering other half, who grabbed him from behind in an affectionate choke hold.

Enough! Neil thought he would gag any second. But he was without weapons, doomed to psychological meltdown at the hands of his torturers. If only Jessica were here! She would keep him sane. Together the two of them would cut the team to shreds, satirizing their pathetic ways until they—Neil and Jessica—were busting their guts with that healing, all-powerful remedy for looming insanity: laughter.

Jessica! All of a sudden Neil broke into an evil grin. Jessica might be gone, but her legacy lived on in the form of—her tapes! Scrambling through the glove compartment with his free hand, Neil found what he was looking for, the perfect shutter-upper, the ideal party picker-upper. Neil slid the tape into the tape machine and cranked up the volume until it maxed out.

As Karen Carpenter began to chirp about birds suddenly appearing, all arguments ceased and a collective but muffled group moan hummed from the back of the Winnebago—no match for the syrupy boom throbbing through the speakers.

"OK, we get the point! Please, stop!" Tom—or was it Todd?—yelled.

"Not a chance!" Neil yelled back as Rob broke into a guffaw of laughter.

119

"Way to go, music man!" Rob shouted. Neil pasted an angelic smile on his face and lip-synched to the words. "Karen rules!" Rob yelled, hugging himself blissfully and piping away in a falsetto. "Close to youuuuuu!"

"Save us!" Pam squeaked. Neil bobbed his head in time to the music. *That's exactly what I'm doing!* he thought with satisfaction, thanking Karen Carpenter for her peppiness and thanking Jessica for her brilliantly kitsch ideas on road-trip sing-alongs. Now everyone had a new focal point for their anger, and that was just fine by Neil. Unity at last!

"Charlie!" Scott leaped off his beloved Harley-Davidson and practically slammed into Charlie as she pelted down the asphalt in her bare feet and straight into his arms.

"Oh, Scott, I've missed you so much!" Charlie moaned, burying her face in Scott's neck, oblivious to the onlookers milling around Peoria's Midnite Owl RV parking lot. She couldn't care less who was watching or even where she was. At that moment, as she inhaled Scott's familiar, woodsy cologne and felt his iron-strong arms around her waist, time and place were irrelevant. All that mattered was that she felt safe and at home in Scott's arms.

Charlie felt tears of relief and anxiety mix in the back of her throat, and she sniffed, trying to keep the floodgates from bursting. The last couple of days had been too much, too stressful, and she wasn't sure she could last another minute being brave.

"You OK, hon?" Scott said, breaking away gently to study Charlie's face.

"Just—happy," Charlie murmured, quickly brushing tears from her eyes before they spilled onto her cheeks.

"Sure?" Scott eyed her curiously, his kind, intelligent gray eyes narrowing as he stroked her cheek.

I can't lie to him, Charlie thought miserably, looking away from the unflinching honesty of Scott's gaze. *I should tell him I'm feeling weak and teary and wound up.* . . . But why worry Scott with her own vague feelings of anxiety? She didn't know what was wrong with her. She didn't have a clear answer to anything. All she knew was that she'd been feeling out of sorts for a while. Something was wrong, that was for sure. But what?

It could turn out to be nothing more than a silly little travel bug. That plus a severe case of boyfriend sickness—similar to but worse than homesickness, yet perfectly curable when the boyfriend in question was following her across the country to remedy it.

"I'm fine," Charlie reassured Scott, pushing all dark thoughts from her mind. Already she felt better, and as she grabbed Scott's hand, marching him toward the Winnebago and Elizabeth, she almost felt back to her old self, almost felt the old lightness in her step, the strength in her body. Almost—

The word nagged at Charlie like a fuzzy but persistent memory, but she forced it back down where it belonged. She needed to live in the moment and enjoy it for all it was worth. Worry led nowhere, especially when it was ill founded. *Everything's going to work out!* she told herself firmly. Scott was right there, and with him by her side, Charlie knew that she could face anything. Not that she had anything in particular to face . . .

"This music is so cheesy. It makes me want to gag." Ruby rolled her eyes as the Peoria Lounge house band swung into another jazzy love song.

"I like it," Elizabeth replied, silently rebuking Ruby for her snobbery. Or maybe it was just envy—this band had a gig, and Ruby didn't. Either way, although Elizabeth liked Ruby and was impressed by her determination with her music, she didn't like the occasional flashes of arrogance she could see in her friend.

Of course, Elizabeth could empathize with being on the sidelines, waiting for something others seemed to have. Like now! Elizabeth's eyes followed Scott and Charlie on the dance floor, holding each other close, oblivious to everyone else in the room. It was hard not to be jealous of them. Scott was so great with Charlie, really sensitive and affectionate, and naturally Charlie adored him too. *But I'm not jealous just because they have something I don't,* Elizabeth reasoned. Jealousy was a useless emotion, and the sooner Ruby realized it, the more positive she'd feel about her own life.

What baloney! Elizabeth blinked, disgusted to realize she'd just spent the last few minutes fooling herself, trying to make out that she was above her feelings. *I'm only human,* she acknowledged, sighing wistfully as she watched other happy couples on the dance floor, staring into each other's eyes as the singer crooned about true love in her smoky, jazzy voice. Naturally Elizabeth didn't begrudge Charlie and Scott or any of the other couples their happiness, but at the same time it was hard not to covet what they had, especially since she'd hoped to have it herself. . . .

Pity I picked the wrong guy to pin my wishes onto, Elizabeth thought ruefully as she watched Sam carousing with Josh and Uli at the bar. He hadn't said a word to her since the Pony Express event, and although she'd wised up to his act and resolved to move on—finally—it still angered her that Sam felt he could treat her so rudely.

"Let's get out of here," Ruby suggested. "It's getting claustrophobic, don't you think?"

"Couldn't agree more," Elizabeth replied, slinging her pocketbook over her shoulder.

"You wanna dance?"

Elizabeth whirled around to find Sam behind her. Despite herself Elizabeth couldn't help feeling a little weak at the sight of him, a strip of taut, brown stomach exposed by his faded turquoise tee and baggy cargo pants. And he wanted to dance. With her. Her mind raced with memories

123

of the last time they'd danced together. . . .

But Elizabeth caught herself just in time. She'd danced to Sam's tunes long enough.

"I don't think so," Elizabeth shot back frostily. "You had your chance, and you blew it!"

"Ouch! No need to flip your lid, Liz. I wasn't actually asking you to dance, just observing," Sam replied smoothly, a derisive smile curling at the corners of his mouth. "You've been staring at the dance floor for so long, I thought I'd come and confirm the obvious, out of human interest."

"Oh, really?" Elizabeth spat. "What, are you writing a report on me?"

"Just making a joke, actually," Sam replied, backing away with his hands in the air.

"How amusing!" Elizabeth's eyes flashed steel blue with rage. "Ruby, weren't we just leaving? I believe I've had enough fun for one night!"

Seething with rage, her eyes blazing, Elizabeth marched out of the club. *At least I finally know where I stand!* she fumed. She was just the butt of Sam's cruel jokes. And there was no mixed message in that. At last all the cards were spread on the table, with Sam the self-declared joker of the pack. But once again the joke was on Elizabeth.

Chapter Nine

"Good game, guys!" Sam panted, wiping sweat from his brow and tossing the basketball into Uli's hands. "But I'm beat. Later, everyone."

Sam downed half a bottle of water in one gulp as he left the courts and strolled back to the Winnebago. His muscles ached, but in a good way. *The perfect Sunday!* Sam mused with a tired smile. For once nobody's nerves were on edge. It seemed everyone was taking advantage of some much needed downtime, and with the girls off shopping and exploring the town and the guys kicking back and playing a couple games of ball, the atmosphere felt a lot less charged than it had in weeks. Thank God!

Sam thought if he had one more run-in with Elizabeth, he would freak once and for all. It had been a pretty hairy few days, and things couldn't have gotten worse than they had last night. *The girl's a loose cannon!* Sam thought, toweling off his neck as he approached the Winnebago. He'd only been trying to patch things up with Elizabeth, but asking her to dance was like asking to get your head bitten off.

He should have known better. But it didn't really matter. Sam stripped to his boxers and tossed off his T-shirt. He felt exhausted and perfectly relaxed. He was alone, and after weeks of too much noise and too many people in each other's faces, the empty Winnebago felt like a palace. No one around, and nothing to do but take a long, hot shower, flop down on a bed, and decompress with a good book. Sam yawned in sleepy satisfaction, hooking his thumbs into the waistband of his boxers. *Maybe I'll take a short nap too. . . .*

"Uh, stop right there, please! This isn't a locker room, in case you haven't noticed."

"Sorry," Sam mumbled with a weak smile. "Didn't notice you there."

"How unusual," Elizabeth muttered under her breath, her cheeks flaming red. She sat up on the fold out she'd been resting on. "You could have looked around before putting on your little strip show!" she added hotly. So much for peace and quiet. All Elizabeth had wanted was a moment to herself, but apparently that was hoping for too much as far as Sam Burgess was concerned.

"Aren't you supposed to be out shopping?" Sam retorted irritably.

"I changed my mind." Elizabeth's stomach flipped with a mixture of outrage and embarrassment. It wasn't her fault that Sam had decided to get naked in her presence, but once again he was trying to put her on the spot for his own thoughtlessness! Why couldn't he just stay out of her way?

"Look, Liz . . ." Sam trailed off and then cleared his throat. "Liz," he began again quietly, "I'm sorry you're so mad at me, but I think you're a little out of line. If anything, I should be mad at you for snubbing me last night."

"Really!" The guy was too much! "Tell me something, Sam, since we're on the subject of last night, where do you get off making jokes at my expense?"

"I was only trying to defuse the situation," Sam replied calmly. "When you laid into me for being so presumptuous as to ask her ladyship to dance, I had to save face. So I did."

Elizabeth's eyes glittered with fury. What a load of crud! Did Sam honestly expect her to sit back and swallow this? "You listen here, Sam. I don't need your attitude, and I'm not going to take it anymore, so lay off!"

"Right back at you, blondie!" Sam folded his arms as Elizabeth folded hers, their eyes locked into a silent war.

But although she sat stone-faced, Elizabeth's

emotions were in turmoil. Was it possible she had overreacted to Sam or misread his intentions? Was she being too hard on him? It was possible. Elizabeth had been so wired ever since Jessica's disappearance. Perhaps some of that worry and frustration was spilling over onto her relationship with Sam. . . .

"Look, I know I'm not perfect, Elizabeth, but could you give me a little breathing room here? I'm sorry if you got the wrong idea at the club, but I wasn't trying to insult you."

Elizabeth narrowed her eyes. Was this just another setup? Or maybe she was being paranoid. Sam certainly sounded sincere, and he looked uncomfortable enough. And Elizabeth had to admit she had a tendency to oversensitivity—not that it wasn't justified. Sam had hurt her before, and it was only smart to be on the lookout.

"OK, I'll give you the benefit of the doubt," Elizabeth conceded. "But for the record, I think you deserved a little slap in the face last night."

"I'll go with that." Sam broke into a relieved smile. "So, are we even now?" he added tentatively.

"I guess," Elizabeth replied coolly. No need to get all warm and fuzzy. After all, they had a long way to go before Elizabeth could trust Sam even as a friend. Especially since he'd pulled her strings many, many times before.

"What's up, peoples?" Josh boomed loudly as he, Uli, and Mickey James stormed into the RV.

"Having a little powwow?" he added with a wink at Sam, yanking open the refrigerator door.

"Would you mind not tracking dirt all the way into the kitchen?" Elizabeth replied coldly. Trust Josh to swagger in on a delicate moment.

"Touchy, touchy." Josh chuckled, elbowing Sam. "Looks like we rescued you just in time, pal. Or did I already miss the fireworks?"

"You missed some," Sam admitted to the grinning guys.

"But not all!" Elizabeth shot back, leaping to her feet. Once again Sam was making fun of her in public, using her as fuel for some frat-boy-level humor. Well, he could forget it! The truce was off!

"Why don't you all pull up a seat," Elizabeth shouted, tears stinging her eyes as she heard Josh snickering.

"Cool off, Liz," Josh said. "I'm just—joshing ya! Ha ha!"

The guys broke into laughter. Elizabeth felt like a balloon that was about to burst. This was truly pathetic. And there was Sam, going along with the guys, jeering with the rest of the chauvinists.

Speechless with anger, Elizabeth walked calmly to the door. But once out of the Winnebago, her face crumpled and she dissolved into tears. *Why did I ever agree to this stupid road trip?* Elizabeth asked herself, walking faster and faster through the parking lot. What was the point? Jessica was lost, and Sam treated her like a dish towel. What was she doing here?

"Liz! Wait!" Sam's voice was far away, but Elizabeth broke into a sprint. All she wanted was to be alone, far away from everyone associated with Intense Coast-to-Coast. And especially far away from Sam.

"Helloooo? Operator?" Jessica queried, rolling her eyes as she was put on hold yet again. Jessica leaned against the pay-phone booth and waved at Elvis, waiting for her in the Caddy with the patience of Job. It had taken ages just to get ICSN's head-office number and then aeons to get through to anyone on the Coast-to-Coast staff, which proved to be the most infuriating part of all. The intern—or whatever underling position she held—apparently didn't even know who Jessica Wakefield was! Thankfully the pinhead eventually realized she was dealing with a celebrity and cleaned up her act, giving Jessica a cell-phone number for Coast-to-Coast field producer Ned Jackson.

But Ned's phone was busy, and Jessica was forced to hang around chewing on the end of Elvis's phone card while the operator continued trying to get through. Any other time Jessica wouldn't have bothered with this dull performance, but she had to speak to Elizabeth and let her sister know she was OK.

"Helloooo?" Jessica repeated. "Idiot!" she muttered sulkily.

"Yes, hello, miss," a chilly voice replied. "Your party's been reached."

Jessica's heart leaped exultantly. "It's me, Jessica!" she shouted into the phone.

"Who?" It was a man, but not Ned.

"Jessica Wakefield!" Jessica snapped, irritated to be wasting yet more valuable time.

"I'm sorry, who would you like to speak with?"

"The queen of England! Who do you think? Ned Jackson, obviously. This is his phone, isn't it?"

"I'm sorry, Mr. Jackson's tied up right now. But if you leave your name, I'll tell him you called."

"I just gave you my name!" Jessica shook her head in disbelief. What did it take to speak to a responsive, intelligent individual who could gauge the strength of her crisis and act accordingly? If she had to wade through this sea of inadequacy for yet another minute, she knew she would flip her lid!

"Look, are you a local volunteer or something?" Jessica queried disparagingly. "Because you obviously don't know what's going down. This is extremely urgent. Put me on to a crew member. Someone who knows who I am!" she added hotly. "And make it fast!"

"OK, OK, keep your pants on," the voice replied with a chuckle. "Just a second." *That's more like it!* Jessica thought, congratulating herself on her assertiveness. She had no patience for bottom-of-the-food-chain half-wits, and she didn't feel the slightest bit bad about it either.

"Hello? Jessica?" Ned! Finally! Jessica almost crowed with delight at the sound of a recognizable voice, and she poured out her request to Ned in a rush of words, stalling his questions and begging him to find Elizabeth.

"You're in luck," Ned answered. "I happen to be standing not ten feet away from her. We're doing a piece on your sister. Sort of a profile on courage, you might say, highlighting the fighting spirit and sense of teamwork she displayed in Missouri," he explained. "We might even air it as a special."

"Yes, yes, very nice," Jessica said irritably. She hadn't called to hear about some Liz love fest. "Ned, as you might imagine, I don't have time to chat," Jessica continued in a snippy voice. "It took me hours just to get your key grip, or whoever it was, to let me talk to you, so if you don't mind . . ."

"Sure," Ned replied, laughing. "Just a second. Oh, and by the way, Jessica, the man you just spoke to was actually the CEO of ICSN. He popped down for a visit, and his mobile cut out, so he's been using mine."

Yikes! Jessica clapped a hand over her mouth, but before she had time to cringe, she heard Elizabeth's eager voice.

"Jess! Thank goodness you called. I've been so worried!"

"I know, and I'm really, really sorry, Liz." Jessica's eyes filled with tears when she heard the strain in Elizabeth's voice. "I just needed my space. Things got pretty hectic. . . ."

Jessica poured out her story, expecting Elizabeth to come down on her with at least one judgmental comment. But to her surprise, Elizabeth merely listened sympathetically and even seemed to understand.

"I just want you to come back," Elizabeth replied once Jessica had finished explaining how she'd been left behind in South Dakota. "I really miss you. Everyone does."

"Not everyone, I'm sure," Jessica retorted humorlessly.

"Things are mellowing out. You'll see when you get here," Elizabeth answered. "Just make sure you do, OK? We'll be in Chicago tomorrow, and Jess? I need you. I'm counting on you to make it."

"Uh . . . ," Jessica began, but she was interrupted by Ned.

"Sorry to cut it short, but we need to wrap the shoot," he said.

"Just give me another minute. . . ." Jessica was met with a static reply.

Stupid mobile phones! Jessica fumed, slamming the receiver onto the hook. But maybe it was just as well. Talking to Elizabeth had made everything seem both better and worse at the same time. Of course it would be great to see her sister, but what about the rest of the gang? Elizabeth knew her twin was OK, and that had been a huge part of Jessica's worry, but now . . . ? Jessica bit her thumbnail anxiously. Would there really be a welcome party to greet her after a long trip to Chicago? Jessica doubted it. And if there wasn't, why was she even going back? Maybe there was already too much water under the bridge. Maybe going back now would be an even bigger mistake than staying put.

Chapter Ten

"OK, guys, listen up!" Richie Valentine boomed as the teams gathered around him at Wrigley Field. "As you can see, event five is gonna be a fun one. It's the Chicago Cubs against the Los Angeles Dodgers out there on the playing field, and you four teams against each other. Now, are you ready to hear what you have to do to win this event?"

Jess, where are you? Elizabeth glanced anxiously around, skimming past hundreds of faces in search of one identical to her own. But it was no use. With a sinking feeling in her stomach, Elizabeth knew Jessica wasn't coming. She'd suspected as much when they'd all arrived in Chicago yesterday and Ned's phone had remained silent all night. And today, Tuesday, it was time for the fifth event and still not a peep from Jessica.

"OK, teams," Richie continued, and Elizabeth

tried to concentrate as he pointed at several hot-dog stands and explained the mission: to sell as many hot dogs as possible. Whichever team sold the most hot dogs and could hand in the cash to prove it scored the highest. "And remember, guys, buying and eating your own dogs doesn't count, but sabotaging other teams by eating theirs is totally admissible," Richie finished with a wicked grin. "Good luck, and may the best vendors win! Heh heh!"

Richie's lame attempt at humor only made Elizabeth feel lower. As she reluctantly walked toward her team to huddle, she could barely muster any of the positive vibe she'd tried to bring to Wrigley Field. *I tried.* . . . Elizabeth lowered her head, crestfallen. She'd overcome so much on this trip, but Jessica's no-show had hit her in the gut more forcefully than anything Sam had done to her. Her sister had abandoned her!

Elizabeth knew Jessica hadn't meant to hurt her by not showing and that she'd probably call from some bizarre little town in Texas to apologize. But that wasn't enough. Elizabeth needed her twin's moral support and upbeat attitude now more than ever—and Jessica knew that. Elizabeth had told Jessica she needed her, that she was counting on her. *She should have come, if not for herself, then for me,* Elizabeth reflected bitterly. But she hadn't. Yet another betrayal from someone who ought to care.

No choice but to keep going. Mechanically

Elizabeth donned an apron and turned to her teammates, forcing all thoughts of Jessica from her mind. "So, what's the strategy?" she asked.

It was all about the game now. Between Jessica's and Sam's independent betrayals, Elizabeth had wasted enough time and energy on losing battles. It was time to harden her heart. It was time to win.

"Thanks, pal!" Todd grinned, accepting yet another pile of quarters as he handed two hot dogs to a small boy dressed in a mini–Cubs uniform. Of course, selling dogs didn't really matter to Team One. Minus Jessica, they still weren't officially back in the running. But who cared? Coast-to-Coast had decided to let the team participate in the fun, and competition aside, Todd was really enjoying himself. *And isn't that what life's all about?* he thought happily.

After all, he was at Wrigley Field, watching the Dodgers, and for a baseball fan that wasn't a bad way to spend a day—even if he couldn't cheer for his favorite team in front of all the bleacher bums roaring for their beloved Cubs. That was tough, but Todd could handle it, especially since there was a chance Jessica might even show and make all his hard work worth it! Rumor had it she was planning to turn up. . . . But either way, Todd didn't really care. He was in his element, infected by the excitement running through the crowd. Nothing could bring him down now.

Except perhaps a star move by Sam Burgess. Todd's face darkened as he watched Sam pull a fast one on a group of preteen girls, getting them to buy up half a crate's worth of dogs just by sweet-talking them. *Jerk!* Todd silently cursed Sam. He'd never liked the guy, and today was proving Sam to be even more of a loser. *Showing his true colors!* Todd mused disapprovingly, taking in Sam's blue-and-white Cubs outfit. The guy was an out-and-out traitor. Selling hot dogs with a little fake Cubs endorsement was one thing, but a California man actually impersonating the enemy—that was sacrilegious!

I'll show him! Todd raced over to an ICSN cameraman and whipped a microphone right out of his hand. Before the guy had a second to react, Todd wrapped a hot-dog bun around the mike and then got to work on his "hat"—spearing a wiener with a straw and poking it through an upside-down plastic-foam cup. *Here goes!* Todd grinned foolishly as people around him began to laugh and cheer. *Everyone loves a fool,* he thought, satisfied.

It certainly looked that way. A crowd began lining up the minute Todd put the cup on his head. "Who wants a hot dog?" Todd yelled through his wiener mike.

"Yeah!" the crowd roared back, and Todd felt his spirits soar with their voices. What a blast!

"Who loves the Cubs?" Todd shouted, squashing

the twinge of guilt he felt as the crowd roared back at him. What he was doing was technically OK, he rationalized, and not the same as dressing up like the real thing. Plus the Dodgers seemed to be doing just fine with or without Todd's active support.

Just then the Dodgers' Jim Bowman made an incredible save, diving back into a shoestring catch. Could the moment be any more complete? Todd stood openmouthed and felt a pull of patriotic fervor. What a rush to see his home team making such headway!

"All right, Dodgers! Whoo-hoo!" Todd yelled gleefully into the microphone. "You guys rock!"

"What a dork!" Todd snapped around to catch a disgusted group of Cubs fans sneering at him.

"Hey, wait!" Todd cried as the line in front of him dissolved as quickly as it had formed.

Loser! Todd smacked a hand to his head and groaned, knocking his "hat" to the ground. Cheering for the Dodgers at Wrigley? Real smart move! He couldn't believe he'd let himself go like that! He'd simply gotten swept away with excitement.

Disgusted, Todd kicked his plastic-foam hat. He wouldn't be needing that anymore.

"C'mon, guys, how about buying from me!" Elizabeth implored a group of teenage boys, but they walked right past her to Sam. *I guess I shouldn't care since we're on the same team,* she thought. Still, Elizabeth was disappointed with her performance. She'd barely made a sale all day.

"You don't want to buy from this lovely lady?" Sam queried with a chuckle as the boys handed him a roll of bills. "Liz, why don't you give them a run for their money?"

"What do you mean?" Elizabeth retorted suspiciously.

"Trust me on this one, OK?" Sam stage-whispered.

Trust him? Was he kidding? But before Elizabeth could say a word, Sam went on, "If we work together, we can double our sales."

"Oh yeah? And what makes you think I want to work with you?"

"You are my teammate, aren't you?" Sam grinned ghoulishly, blue-and-white war paint coloring his lips.

Elizabeth couldn't dispute that fact. Nor could she dispute Sam's ability to sell. Maybe she should cash in on his expertise. After all, she could use a little help from anyone ready to give it—even Sam.

Elizabeth nodded. "OK!" Sam cleared his throat and pulled Elizabeth toward him. "Who wants to buy a hot dog from this beautiful lady? It's only a dollar, and you get a kiss along with your dog!"

"Me!" the boys chanted, clustering around Elizabeth, lascivious grins revealing mouths full of metal and rubber bands.

"What?" Elizabeth recoiled as if Sam had just held a blowtorch to her skin. "Do you think I'm a piece of meat?" she hissed indignantly.

"They're just a bunch of kids," Sam argued. "What do you say, Liz? For the good of the team? You know we need the points."

Again Sam was right. And although she dreaded the thought of planting her lips on a bunch of pimply fourteen-year-old cheeks, she knew she'd look like a wuss if she got too precious about the whole thing.

"Fine," Elizabeth declared, stepping up to the group of boys. "Show me the money!" she demanded, enjoying Sam's surprise, which he was trying unsuccessfully to hide. *He thought I'd back out,* Elizabeth realized, gloating. Maybe he'd even wanted her to, just so he could show her up in front of a crowd. *Unfortunately for him, I'm tougher than he thinks!*

Elizabeth plucked a row of bills from the sweaty palms of several overexcited boys and surveyed the crowd coolly. The prospect was ugly, but Elizabeth's eyes were on the prize: another win for Team One and a personal triumph over Sam. It was worth it.

Pocketing the money, Elizabeth gave Sam a tight, victorious smile and then turned back to the teens.

"Who's first?"

*　　　*　　　*

141

What the heck is going on? Tom tried to catch a glimpse of whatever tricks Sam was pulling to attract such a crowd, but all he could see was a wave of bodies and fistfuls of dollar bills being thrust into the air. Not a good sign.

Knowing Burgess, he was putting on a big show for everyone, including Elizabeth. Tom's face tightened in anger. Sure, there was trouble in paradise—you could drag a knife through the tension between Sam and Elizabeth, especially since the Pony Express event—but Tom was convinced the moody-wild-man act was all just a part of Sam's grand master plan to make Elizabeth his own.

Think, Watts! He had to come up with a snappy idea, something to steal the glory away from Sam and impress Elizabeth. And whatever it was, it would have to be a whole lot cooler and more glamorous than simply stealing a bunch of hot dogs from Team Three and eating them, which was all he'd been doing for the past hour. Tom felt sick at the thought of eating another hot dog. *The way to Elizabeth's heart is definitely not through my stomach!* he joked weakly, racking his brains for ideas that wouldn't come.

"And folks, once again we're coming at you live!" Richie Valentine began. "The heat is on now," he continued as the cameras panned to capture the teams at work. "But it looks like something—or someone—is drawing the crowds to Team Two! Hopefully we'll soon find out their secret," Richie continued as several cameramen threaded their way through the bleachers to get to Team Two's zone.

Great! Tom thought glumly. Things were getting even worse. Unless he came up with something good, something that showed he was the better man, Sam would bask in live-TV limelight!

Unless . . . Suddenly Tom's pulse quickened as his eyes flicked over to the giant stadium screen, the grinning mugs of Cubs fans plastered all over it in hundreds of feet of pixelated vision. There was no doubt about it, this was an opportunity of gigantic proportion—and an opportunity Tom fully intended to turn to his advantage.

Maximum exposure, maximum effect. Tom always told WSVU trainee reporters to remember that adage.

Perhaps it was time to put those words to the test.

"My turn!" a chubby boy screeched as his friends pushed him toward Elizabeth.

Elizabeth rolled her eyes as Sam grinned, but even she couldn't help a smile. The ploy was definitely working. The bucks were rolling in faster than she could pucker her lips, and all the silliness was actually kind of fun.

"As I said before, you're the money, Liz!" Sam joked.

"You've got that right!" Elizabeth replied, expertly applying Chapstick to her dry, overused lips as the line before her swelled with eager males. It seemed half the stadium's population was emptying their wallets for kissing money, especially during breaks between innings, like now.

"OK, time-out! She's taking a break," Sam cut in suddenly, blocking Elizabeth's next customer, a chiseled, six-foot college-age guy with spiky black hair and intelligent eyes. Elizabeth felt a bubble of laughter rise up in her throat and escape into a loud guffaw.

"You're jealous!" She snickered.

"I am not!" Sam scoffed weakly. "And hey, isn't that Tom up there?" he added, pointing at the giant stadium screen.

"Don't try and change the subject by making things up!" Elizabeth teased. "I know you're—"

"Seriously! Look!"

Something in Sam's voice made Elizabeth snap her head around, and sure enough, there was Tom, beaming in front of the entire stadium. What was he up to? Something about Tom's manic, rather absurd grin gave Elizabeth a bad feeling.

"Hi, everyone, I'm Tom Watts, and I'm an Intense Cable Sports Network Coast-to-Coast participant! Thank you," he added, as a smattering of applause broke out from a few pockets around the stadium. "I've got a special message for one of my fellow road trippers. Well, for two, actually: Elizabeth Wakefield and Sam Burgess!"

"What's this all about?" Elizabeth hissed as Sam shrugged. *Whatever it is, thank goodness no one knows who I am!* Elizabeth reassured herself.

"Elizabeth Wakefield is right up there on tier four. She's wearing an orange ICSN T-shirt, and she's the most beautiful blond hot-dog vendor in the world!"

Elizabeth cringed as the crowd around her craned their necks and pointed.

"Elizabeth, I know we aren't on the same team, and I know you're on the same team with Sam, the man of many tricks. But although this competition divides us into rival hot-dog-selling teams, I come to you with something else, something Sam Burgess doesn't have, something he can't give you."

And what could that possibly be? Elizabeth closed her eyes for a moment, dreading the answer even more than she loathed being singled out in front of thousands of strangers.

"Liz," Tom boomed, his face growing more serious, "in front of all these people gathered here today, I want to tell you how I feel!"

Oh no! Elizabeth gasped as ripples of laughter echoed rapidly through the crowd. What kind of hokey stunt was this? And since when had Tom developed into some kind of cheesy, talk-show guest, airing his private feelings for a mass of voyeurs?

"My heart is on my sleeve, Liz," Tom continued, "and although I may not be the hottest dog, I think you'll agree, my buns are better! Camera, close-up, please!"

Tell me this isn't happening! Elizabeth prayed as

Tom spun around, dropped his pants to reveal blue-and-white candy-striped boxers, and wiggled his rear end to the collective boos of the crowd!

"And you dated this guy?" Sam mumbled, apparently as shattered as everyone else by Tom's mortifying, big-screen display.

"Don't remind me," Elizabeth murmured, her face a glowing, tomato red. "Right now I can't believe it myself!" How could Tom have done this to her? *He doesn't care about me—this is just a stupid competition between Tom and Sam!* Elizabeth thought bitterly, her eyes blazing with anger.

"It's her!"

Elizabeth looked down to see a cameraman zoom in on her. Too late she realized what was going on, and slowly, filled with horror, she lifted her eyes to the screen to meet her own gaze.

Dumbfounded, Elizabeth could only stare at her giant, larger-than-life-sized self staring back at her with helpless, larger-than-life-sized terror. And then, in a sickening split second of realization, it dawned on her how bad things really were. Not only was she gracing the screen, her reaction in full view of thousands of people in the stadium, but she was also on millions of tiny screens all across the country. Millions!

National humiliation! It was too much to bear, and since the earth hadn't done her the favor of opening up and swallowing her whole, Elizabeth did the only other thing she could. She ran.

Chapter Eleven

"Ever seen a guy juggle five hot-dog buns at once?" Neil questioned two giggling kids as they passed his hot-dog stand.

"Nope," they replied in unison, watching him eagerly.

"Me either!" Neil muttered gloomily, taking off his baseball cap and wiping his perspiring forehead with a napkin. The kids shrugged and moved on, and Neil drained the remnants of a Mountain Dew. He was more than exhausted by the effort he'd put in trying to sell hot dogs, and although he'd done OK, the Oscar Mayer experience was beginning to wear a little thin.

Why am I busting my gut? Neil thought irritably. Between Todd's idiotic Dodgers patriotism and Tom's mind-numbing big-screen faux pas, Team One had done enough to alienate every last Cubs fan. As Elizabeth yakked away to the cameramen and flipped her hair a dozen times, Neil frowned. Since when did Elizabeth put on such a show for the cameras—and since when had she changed into that tight, cherry red minidress?

Suddenly it hit him with the force of a line drive to the head. Jessica! She'd made it! Neil could barely contain his excitement and relief. Not only was Team One back in the running, but obviously Jessica had forgiven him, or else she wouldn't have come back!

Neil sprinted toward Jessica with an ear-to-ear grin. "Hey, Jess!" he yelled as he came within earshot.

But instead of a welcoming smile, Jessica acknowledged him with only a slight inclination of her head. *Guess I spoke too soon,* Neil concluded grimly. Judging by Jessica's brush-off, he could tell she still resented him.

"So, why did you leave?" Richie Valentine queried importantly, thrusting his mike under Jessica's nose.

Uh-oh! Neil froze in his tracks as Jessica opened her mouth to answer. *Don't tell!* Neil begged silently, but he could see by the look on Jessica's face that his feelings didn't matter anymore. She was angry, and maybe too angry to take the heat for him any longer.

"I left for a very good reason," Jessica began slowly as Neil willed her to have some last-minute

148

mercy. *She'll cover for me!* Neil told himself as his hands turned to ice. *She wouldn't out me on national television—would she?*

"A very good reason, ah, yes," Jessica rambled as she struggled to think of a way to exonerate herself. This was her chance to tell her side of the story! Jessica's mind raced. She had to come up with a good answer, had to make her leaving the team seem less reprehensible than everyone no doubt thought it was. *Maybe honesty is the best policy,* she thought, biting her lip and taking a deep breath.

"Jessica?" Richie prompted.

The truth shall set me free! But as she opened her mouth, Neil's pleading eyes power-drilled through her heart. Although Jessica knew that protecting Neil would come at her expense, she couldn't bring herself to spill his secret.

"If you must know, I left the team because I needed some time to myself," Jessica replied breezily. "You viewers might not know it, but life on the road isn't all it's cracked up to be! You try blow drying your hair in a bathroom the size of a soap dish," Jessica joked halfheartedly as Neil mouthed a grateful thank-you from behind Richie.

"So, you're saying being a teamster isn't your bag, Jessica?" Richie continued as Jessica fidgeted uncomfortably. *How the heck am I supposed to answer that one? Now everyone thinks I'm a total*

149

flake! Jessica reflected miserably. Not even her most winning, most Marilyn Monroe–esque smile would charm her out of this mess and make her look better than the team ditcher they all thought she was. Also, Team One was beginning to look like Loserville, and Jessica would have to shoulder the blame once again. It just wasn't fair!

"Actually, I love being a teamster," Jessica lied. "As you can see, I missed my teammates so much, I simply had to come back. Why, it's precisely because of this fabulous gang that I'm prepared to withstand the deprivation of the Winnebago lifestyle."

"Good for you, Jessica!" Richie chuckled. "As you can see, folks, our Coast-to-Coasters have that fighting spirit. And although the impulse to desert can seem alluring at times, our kids are happiest when they're together!"

Puh-leeze! Jessica thought, but she merely smiled in agreement, a smile so wide, she thought her face might crack with the effort. And things were getting even worse. Neil was coming toward her with open arms. Like she could deal with that right now.

"Jess! I missed you so much," Neil murmured as he enfolded her in a hug. "I'm so relieved you're back," he added, tightening his arms around her waist.

"Me too," Jessica replied stiffly. Did Neil really want bygones to be bygones, or was this hug just for the benefit of the cameras? Either way, Jessica felt as if her emotions were being put through a blender.

"Looks like you've been missed too, Jessica," Richie commented with an annoying wink. "Can we safely say we've made a Coast-to-Coast love connection here?"

"Of course not!" Neil blurted out, letting go of Jessica as if she were a leper he'd accidentally touched.

Well, thanks a lot! Jessica glared at Neil, turned on her heel, and pushed past the cameras. *Looks like somebody did get embarrassed on national television after all!* she thought miserably, tears prickling her eyes. Why had she bothered to protect Neil's feelings when he couldn't even give her the same respect? And why did she even bother to come back? A whole day on the bus for this!

That's it! I'm outta here! Jessica forced her way through the crowds, her eyes firmly fixed on the exit. She would go where she was wanted and where she got the appreciation she deserved. Of course, it was a ten-hour trip back to Memphis, but Jessica didn't care. She'd wasted one day already. What difference would one more make?

How am I ever going to live this down? Elizabeth groaned. She could barely wrap her head around Tom's galling stunt. But she could easily picture the jokes that would be told in its aftermath. *Sam will go to town on this one,* Elizabeth thought bleakly as she fought her way toward the exit. No question about it, this was the last straw in a week of last straws. For as long as she continued with Coast-to-Coast, she would be a walking target for any number of hot-dog-related jokes. And that was way more than she could cope with.

As she neared the exit, Elizabeth's throat constricted with the force of all the tears she'd been holding back, but she refused to give in to her emotions. Not until she was far, far away. . . .

"Liz?"

Elizabeth refused to even turn her head. She couldn't face dealing with Charlie or Ruby right now. They would simply try to talk her into staying. *Not now!* The two words spun around and around in her head until they became like a motivational chant to get her through that door and away from all the staring faces.

"Liz!"

"Please, I just need to be—" The words died on Elizabeth's lips as she looked up to see Jessica suddenly in front of her.

"I can't believe it!" Elizabeth murmured, clinging to Jessica as if she were a life preserver. "You're really here!"

"Not for much longer," Jessica replied bitterly.

The sisters spilled their stories to each other, half laughing, half crying at the coincidence of their double national humiliation.

"Oh, well, at least we spiced up the stupid Intense broadcast," Jessica reflected, squeezing Elizabeth's shoulder comfortingly.

"No one can say we bore our audience," Elizabeth admitted, wadding a soggy tissue into a ball. "America will be talking about us until the cows come home. Me especially!"

"Oh, come on, Liz, it's not that bad. So you're queen of the wiener serenade! Who cares? Tom's the one who really comes out looking like a turnip."

Maybe Jessica is right, Elizabeth thought. *And maybe I'm making a mountain out of a molehill.* She sighed. This trip was making her crazy. Since when did she get into such dramatic situations anyway? And even then, the old Elizabeth would have dealt calmly with the situation, not flounced off like—like Jessica Wakefield!

"I say we get back in there," Elizabeth proposed, grabbing Jessica's arm with determination.

"Hold your horses, Liz! I wasn't saying—"

"Well, I am!" Elizabeth interrupted. "Do we want all of America to think the Wakefield girls are quitters?"

Jessica chewed her lip thoughtfully. "I guess not," she said doubtfully, "but—"

"No buts—and yes, you are!" Elizabeth insisted, linking her arm through Jessica's. "Did you come all this way for nothing?"

"No," Jessica replied in a small voice.

"Good, because neither did I. Now, let's get back in there and sell those darned hot dogs. OK? And don't worry, if anyone so much as looks at us the wrong way, I'll snap them like a twig!"

"Yes, sir!" Jessica smiled, eyeing her sister shrewdly. "Wow, Liz, you're so powerful all of a sudden. And since when did you become such a diva anyway?" she quipped, giggling.

"Since someone had to fill your shoes," Elizabeth jibed.

"Well, cut it out 'cause I'm back!"

We both are! Elizabeth thought with satisfaction, confidence surging through her with every step. *And we'll show them all!*

Chapter Twelve

"And it's a winning round for Team Three here at Wrigley!" Richie announced enthusiastically. "Unfortunately, guys, you're still bringing up the rear overall! Fifty points notwithstanding, you're behind even our Team One here. Yes, folks, Jessica Wakefield's surprise 'home run' unfortunately turned out to be too little, too late, for Team One. Not enough players meant yet another no score for them this time round. . . ."

Drop dead, tubby! Neil scowled as Richie continued his irritating patter. Jessica's "home run"! The guy thought he was hilariously funny, but Neil knew Richie's thoughtless jokes were like rubbing salt into Jessica's wounds. *We'll be lucky if she doesn't split on us again,* he thought.

"But not to worry, Team One! You're still maintaining in third place with 110 points. Not bad, considering the last two disastrous events! In fact, you're not far behind, not far at all. And talk about a close race, folks, our winning place so far goes to Team Four and Team Two. Both split thirty points for their hot-dog sales today, and both are going neck and neck overall, with 130 points per team!"

Neil stole a glance at Jessica and winced as she shot him a black look in response. *I didn't mean it! It was just a joke!* Neil begged silently, but Jessica merely turned her head away in disgust and proceeded to whisper furiously into Elizabeth's ear.

Neil shook his head. What was he supposed to say or do now? Naturally he hadn't meant to make Jessica feel rejected by his automatic response to Richie's stupid question. It was in any case a question both he and Jessica had been asked countless times already by fellow teammates and everyone else who knew they were joined at the hip. And like him, Jessica had also answered in a smart-mouthed way, pretending she couldn't think of anything worse than being with Neil. But that was before. . . . Jessica was hypersensitive now, and Neil could understand why.

Still—couldn't she cut him a little slack? Couldn't she see that hurting her was the furthest thing from his mind?

"All in all, we've had a great time here in Chicago, but it's time to get back on the road. And once again our teams know as little as you do about where they're going and what they're doing next. But we'll be answering the first part of that question just as soon as we've heard from our sponsors."

Neil grimaced as Richie flashed his famous toothy grin. His teeth were so white, they were giving Neil a headache. In fact, the whole trip was giving him a dull, perpetual throbbing at the base of his skull. He just wanted it to be over.

"We're back—but not for long! Folks, our next stop takes us to a place where stars are made. Nope, not Hollywood, California, but Nashville, Tennessee!"

It was all the same to Neil. He couldn't care less where the teams were going next, but Jessica looked brighter. Maybe Jessica had a soft spot for Tennessee?

Neil hoped he was right because it was a long way to Nashville, and he was running low on emotional fuel.

"I'll drive!" Todd announced, throwing on a fresh sweatshirt. As the others climbed into their seats, Todd revved the Winnebago impatiently. Although part of him was dreading the long trip to Nashville—cooped up with a sulky Jessica and a whiny Pam—for the most part he felt relieved to be getting out of Chicago.

Not your best effort, Todd chastised himself. He was still sore about his embarrassing blunder. But thankfully, Team One's overall performance hadn't been affected by him personally, and as Todd hit the open road, he felt a little better. *We could still win this thing,* he told himself. They weren't that far behind, despite his moment of supreme public dorkiness. More to the point, despite Tom's.

Todd glanced at Tom in the seat next to him. Poor guy! He looked so low, even Todd had to sympathize.

"Cheer up, pal," he said. "It wasn't that bad. We were DQ'd because of Jessica anyway, not you."

"Points aside, I think we can safely say I made a major-league mistake—literally and metaphorically," Tom replied gloomily.

"Let it go. We all have," Todd offered magnanimously. Of course, if the team had suffered as a result of Tom's behavior, Todd would have been the first to let him have it. But Team One was in a lot better shape than Tom was personally, and Todd could afford to be generous, even to his nemesis. *He's a teammate, after all,* Todd acknowledged. *And I'm a team-playing kind of guy.*

"I should have drowned myself in a vat of mustard while I had the chance. Or barbecued my head on that hot-dog grill," Tom continued morosely. "I don't know what came over me."

"Quit hauling yourself over the coals," Todd replied. "Sorry, I couldn't resist," he added, chuckling as Tom shot him a cold look. "But seriously, don't beat yourself up about it. You still have plenty of chances to redeem yourself."

"I hope you're right, man." Tom popped open a tube of Pringles and began munching disconsolately, his eyes fixed bleakly on the road ahead. Todd turned up the volume on the car stereo, and Tom seemed to perk up a bit, nodding to the beat.

"The road is long . . . ," Todd sang along, pumping the accelerator. *Yup, it sure is,* he reflected. *In more ways than one.* Fleetingly an image of his girlfriend, Dana Upshaw, came to mind. With her clear skin, thick, mahogany mane of hair, and fiery attitude, Dana was a catch by anyone's standards. But Todd had been looking forward to a break from all the intensity of their relationship, a chance to travel light for a while. And he'd gotten what he'd wanted.

With an ironic smile, Todd hummed along to the rest of the song. It was true that despite all the bumps in the road, Coast-to-Coast wasn't a total disaster. For one thing, it was making him miss Dana, a nice change from the claustrophobia he'd begun to feel around her. And for another thing, Team One stood a good chance of coming out in the green, a wad of cash awaiting each of them for their troubles.

"Just keep your eyes on the prize, Watts," Todd suggested as he switched into the fast lane. *Because I sure am!*

Chapter Thirteen

"Nashville ought to be fun, right, guys?" Neil cajoled as Jessica sat stone-faced next to him.

"Hmmph," Pam retorted from the seat opposite, where she lay curled up across Rob's lap, chewing gum and staring at the ceiling.

For the first time I agree with Frizzball! Jessica thought irritably. Pam wasn't the only one in a mood, and no matter how much Neil was trying, Jessica was having a hard time sharing his enthusiasm. Objectively Jessica could see Neil was doing his best, but his hyperattentiveness, from asking her if she wanted a window seat to offering her a snack every two minutes, was beginning to suffocate her.

It's probably all fake anyway! Jessica concluded, staring woodenly in front of her. Neil might want to make things right between them, but he was going about it all wrong. Like now, acting all excited about Tennessee. What was he? Intense's carnival pitchman?

"Pam, Rob, can I get you guys a soda?"

Since when was Neil so chummy and chipper with everyone? This wasn't the guy Jessica had felt so connected to. *What happened to "us against them"?* Jessica wondered, recalling the way she and Neil had always snickered over Pam and Rob, making witty remarks that flew right over the couple's empty little heads.

Guess I've got some catching up to do, she thought grimly. Everything seemed to have changed in Jessica's absence, and Team One was now one big, happy family, with Neil at the helm, radiating team spirit. It was enough to make Jessica want to throw up.

"So, listen, guys, I was thinking, we really need to pull out all the stops in Memphis. Go all out like Liz did in St. Joseph. Just go for it!" Neil slammed his fist into his palm like some hyperkeen sports coach.

"You know what they say, one percent inspiration, ninety-nine percent perspiration. . . ." Neil bubbled away like a babbling brook of wisdom, and Jessica could barely conceal her distaste. Super-Liz, Super-Liz! Couldn't these people talk about anything else? From Neil to Rob to Pam to Todd, Jessica had heard nothing but praise for Elizabeth's "gutsy moves" from the minute she'd set foot in Chicago. *Like I need reminding.*

Maybe that's the point! Jessica sat up in her seat, her fists clenched in her lap. Perhaps all this Lizspeak was nothing but a veiled insult, a subtle way of making Jessica feel guilty for not doing her part for the team. *Well, they can take their lesson and shove it!* Jessica thought, her cheeks burning with anger.

"I know what you're all up to," Jessica snapped, her eyes narrowing suspiciously as she glared at Neil, then Pam, then Rob. "But before you get all high and mighty about my 'performance,' let me remind you who left whom, OK?"

"What? Who was talking about you? I was talking about Elizabeth," Neil retorted as Pam's eyes widened in anger.

"I know!" Jessica interrupted coldly. "My perfect twin sister. I get it, all right?"

"Well, I don't! Just what exactly are you insinuating, Jessica?" Neil asked, folding his arms defensively.

"I'm insinuating nothing, but you all are!" Jessica spat. "I'd have preferred the silent treatment. It's a lot more honest!"

"I don't know what this is about, but you should get off our backs!" Neil shot back vehemently. "Especially since we're all making an effort to stay off yours!"

"Our backs"—that said it all! It was a conspiracy, or at the very least them against her! But what gave them the right to act like they were so innocent?

"I know you left me behind in South Dakota

163

deliberately," Jessica replied acidly. "I know, OK? That's all I'm saying."

"Oh yeah, of course we did! You're right, Jessica, we left you in Wonderlust on purpose!" Neil yelled. "I can't believe this," he muttered, stalking off to the kitchen.

Well, I can! At least Neil had finally admitted the truth, although it was no big surprise to Jessica. Bleakly she stared out the window, watching the landscape fly by. The Winnebago was so silent, she could almost hear the animosity in the room.

Jessica sighed and leaned her head against the glass windowpane. She'd never felt more trapped in her life. And there were still hours and hours of driving ahead. *Elvis, where are you when I need you most?*

"If it wasn't for that bonehead Burgess, I would never have made such an idiot of myself," Tom admitted, seething. "But I guess I shouldn't have tried to upstage an egomaniac," he added bitterly. "The guy acts like he owns Elizabeth, and he hardly even knows her."

"You said it, Sam is ego supremo." Todd nodded vigorously. "Always hogging the spotlight, thinking he's such a big shot!"

"When in fact he's all surface, zero substance!" Tom chimed in. "I mean, if he really cares about Liz, then why does he act like she's a piece of gum stuck to his shoe?"

"Beats me." Todd shook his head, swiftly overtaking a heavy-duty truck. "Burgess is a slimy player," he agreed. "Did you see him in that Cubs getup? The guy doesn't have a decent bone in his body."

Tom glowered, picturing Sam probably sucking up to Elizabeth right now. Either that or insulting her. What did she see in him? Because evidently she saw something. There was no mistaking the fact that Elizabeth was more than casually interested in everything Sam did or said. Far more interested in Sam than in anything Tom had to offer. *He's a challenge, that's why!* Tom's mouth twisted in disgust. What was it with girls and their attraction to guys who treated them like dirt? And Elizabeth, of all people, to fall for that act? Tom would never have thought she'd be so dumb.

"Liz had better watch out," Todd muttered, echoing Tom's thoughts. "If she doesn't come to her senses soon, she'll be sorry."

"Nothing we can do about it." Tom moaned. "If she wants to scrape the bottom of the barrel, we can't stop her."

"But maybe we can stop him," Todd exclaimed. "Look, it's our duty to protect Liz. She's our friend. We can't just watch her walk off a cliff without doing anything about it."

"OK, what do you suggest?" Tom asked eagerly. He was up for anything that would cut that slimebag Burgess out of the equation.

165

"I'm not sure yet, but I think between the two of us, we can figure something out."

"Hmmm . . ." Tom furrowed his brow, casting about for a plan, something good, something to send Sam a message to stay away from Elizabeth once and for all. *Remember what happened last time you tried to send the guy a message, Watts,* he thought, grimacing. Tom had to concede his strategies weren't exactly brilliant these days. But maybe that was the problem. They were strategies.

"I say we just confront him, pure and simple. No behind-the-scenes plots, just us two facing up to him, letting him know we're watching every move he makes!"

"You mean, threaten him?" Todd said.

"If you want to put it that way. I'm tired of pussyfooting around that punk! I say we tell him exactly what we think, straight up. And the sooner the better."

Tom sat back in his seat, pleased with the way things were going. Todd's attitude cemented Tom's feelings about Sam. And the positive reinforcement was like a tonic after all the self-criticism that had been infesting Tom's mind.

Of course, it was a little weird to be bonding with Todd Wilkins. *We might have a common enemy, but he's still a jerk,* Tom reminded himself. And it was important to bear that in mind. Agreeing was one thing, but friendship? No way!

"Watch your speed, Wilkins," Tom sniped. A

little insult could help dilute all the dangerous buddy vibes zooming around the air.

"Cut the backseat driving, Watts," Todd spat in response. "I'll drive however I want to drive!"

Tom turned his head to watch the fields of corn crops sliding by. *Good,* he thought with a smile. *We understand each other perfectly!*

"I say we push on to Nashville and skip Louisville," Elizabeth suggested, pointing at the map. "We're making such good time, we might as well just get there."

"What's wrong with Louisville?" Sam queried. "It could be fun to hang out for a night. And isn't Team Four staying there?"

"I think we should keep driving," Elizabeth retorted tersely. "Who agrees with me?"

"I don't care," Ruby offered unhelpfully, strumming her guitar.

"Me either." Josh shrugged and rolled his eyes.

"All right, everyone." Sam sighed. "Liz says push on, we push on. My turn to drive." *Of course! What Elizabeth wants, Elizabeth gets!* Sam tried to conceal his irritation and casually hoisted himself into the driver's seat. "Uli, suntan time is over, man," he shouted, honking the horn as Uli reluctantly rolled off the grassy verge at the Mobil Stop-N-Go. "Liz, your turn to shotgun with me."

"No thank you," Elizabeth replied coolly. "I think I'd be more comfortable in the back."

"Maybe the others wouldn't be, though," Sam shot back, unable to resist.

"Yeah? What's that supposed to mean?"

"Simmer down, Liz. Do you have to take everything so seriously? Jeez!" Sam shook his head, and Josh snickered.

"Is this fun for you?" Elizabeth's voice was low and harsh. "Do you get a thrill from attacking me?"

"No, but you seem to like it," Sam replied evenly.

"Whoa, run that by me again?" Elizabeth didn't seem to care that Uli, Ruby, and even Charlie had gathered around.

She wants a scene? Sam thought. *I'll give her a scene!*

"Come on, Liz. You're like a piranha chewing on poor defenseless plankton today. I mean, what's with the big race to get to Nashville? And refusing to ride shotgun with me? I should be the one with the hurt feelings—am I right, guys?" Sam smiled as Josh snickered.

Elizabeth looked as if she was about to slice him from the navel to the neck, but Sam refused to wipe the smile off his face. She'd been tenser than a tightrope walker all day, and although he wasn't about to get all riled up, he wasn't going to take her attacks lying down either.

"I just thought it would be a good idea to get to Nashville so we could all relax and get some space," Elizabeth began in a trembling voice.

"And as for not riding shotgun, I just wanted to lie down for a while."

"That's cool," Sam replied evenly. "But there are ways of saying stuff, Liz, and if you ask me, you've been pulling quite the queen-of-the-Winnebago act lately."

"Excuse me?" Elizabeth's voice quavered, and she blinked, her blue-green eyes shinier than usual. *She's just gearing up for another go!* Sam thought angrily, but he took care not to let his anger show. He was better doing what he knew best. Casual, pointed commentary. From the driver's seat.

"Just an observation, Liz," Sam continued coolly. "Keep your claws in—I'm just an innocent bystander!" he added as Josh snorted, trying to keep back his laughter.

"I'll do you one better," Elizabeth replied quietly. "I'll s-stay out of your way altogether." A tear dripped onto her cheek before she turned and walked away.

That was weird! Sam's smile disappeared abruptly as he watched Elizabeth walk slowly to the back of the Winnebago, her shoulders hunched. He'd been expecting Elizabeth to come back with her usual venom-filled punch line or at least to walk off in an angry huff. But something about her quavering voice and the tear falling onto her cheek caught Sam the wrong way, and his chest suddenly felt tighter than normal.

This isn't like Elizabeth. Did I go too far? Sam

wondered in alarm. He hadn't meant to really wound her, just call her on the way she'd been treating him. Just spar with her like always.

But apparently he'd struck a nerve because he'd never seen Elizabeth so vulnerable. And although he wanted to shrug it off, although he wanted to chalk it up as yet another tiff, Sam knew this time had been different. And he didn't feel good about it. At all.

This is awful! Charlie sank back onto her pillows and took deep breaths as the Winnebago swerved around a corner. She felt as if they'd been on the road for a year, but she still couldn't get used to the never-ending bumping and lurching. And as if all the vibration and noise weren't enough, the tension between Sam and Elizabeth only made it harder to breathe in the cramped quarters.

If only I'd ridden with Scott! Charlie thought miserably, rolling onto her side. But that wasn't allowed. Although Scott was trailing right behind on his motorcycle and although Charlie knew she'd be far more comfortable traveling with the man she loved, ICSN rules dictated that all contestants had to ride in the team RVs.

"You want that I make you a tuna-fish sandwich?" Uli asked kindly, peering around the divider door to check on Charlie. "I am making them for snack."

"Uh, no thanks. I'll stick with water." *Tuna fish. Ugh!* The very thought made Charlie want to get sick. But she forced a smile to her face. "Maybe later," she added with artificial brightness. She didn't want Uli to see how ill she felt because she didn't want anyone else—especially Elizabeth—to fuss all over her and ask her pointed questions about her health.

Questions meant answers, and Charlie didn't have any of those. All she knew was that she'd been having waves of nausea on a daily basis and they hadn't gone away with Scott's arrival. Even being with Scott again hadn't made Charlie suddenly feel more like herself.

It must be the road trip, she told herself for the hundredth time. What else could it be? Charlie leaned over and took a long sip of water. Somewhere inside her she felt other answers bubbling away, but she pushed them back down where they belonged. She was fine. Or she would be fine once all this gallivanting around the country had stopped. It was enough to make anyone dizzy!

But in her heart Charlie knew that wasn't the truth of it. Something like a splinter pricked at her consciousness, began working its way to the surface. But Charlie dismissed it and closed her eyes. She didn't want any answers. Not right now.

Just stay strong! Charlie willed herself, her eyes focusing on the ceiling of the Winnebago. The competition was halfway over, and Charlie knew

171

she had to keep going. It was either that or face the truth and find out what was wrong with her once and for all. But whatever it was, Charlie couldn't cope with it right now.

"Feeling OK, Charlie?" Ruby called out from the kitchen.

"I'm fine. Just reading my book," Charlie replied mechanically, picking up a book and holding it in front of her face. She would have to put on a major act for the next two weeks. She had to, to keep things from falling apart.

You'll get through this, she told herself, staring miserably at the pages of her book. But somehow she wasn't entirely convinced.

"So, I guess we're just outside Owensboro. Right on the border of Kentucky," Josh observed, peering over Sam's shoulder at the map. Team Two were all crowded into a booth at a rest-stop restaurant, waiting out a sudden rain shower.

"We should be in Nashville within the next two hours," Elizabeth commented, trying to keep her tone even. For the last few hours, since her run-in with Sam, she'd felt like disappearing into thin air. Or at the very least crawling up into a ball and crying.

But no matter how excruciatingly difficult it was, Elizabeth knew she had to pull herself together. Any more histrionics would only make the atmosphere in the Winnebago worse and further upset the dynamic of the team. *Sam loathes me, but the rest of the team doesn't have to,* Elizabeth kept telling herself.

Elizabeth had managed to keep her emotions in check by answering questions, taking her turn at the wheel, reading maps—all numbly, like a robot.

Inside, it was a different story. Elizabeth didn't feel angry, like she usually felt after Sam's put-downs. She was beyond anger. Now she felt something stronger than anger—an overwhelming sense of defeated sadness that ate at her heart like hydrochloric acid.

What Sam had done was awful, openly humiliating her in front of every single one of her teammates. But what was worse was knowing that she'd put herself in a combative situation with Sam to begin with. *Why can't I just rise above this nonsense?* she asked herself for the millionth time. *And since when do I let someone else control my emotions like this?*

Elizabeth knew she couldn't plumb the depths of those questions right then, sitting in a damp rest-stop restaurant, but still, they resounded in her mind, basically providing background noise to everything she did or said. There was no doubt— she'd changed these last few weeks on the road, and not for the better either.

"Liz, do you want another soda?" Ruby asked, and Elizabeth blinked herself back to the present.

A waitress was standing in front of her with a notepad.

"No thanks," Elizabeth said quietly. "I—I think I'll just get some air," she added, standing up abruptly. It was all too much. Everyone's eyes were on her, questioningly—everyone's eyes but Sam's since he seemed to be refusing to look at her. The muggy air of the small restaurant was suffocating too, thick with stale grease, unspoken words, and . . . pity! Elizabeth could see it in Ruby's eyes. And Charlie's and Uli's—even Josh's. She had to get out.

"Excuse me," Elizabeth mumbled, stepping past Ruby. *Don't make a scene!* she warned herself as she walked slowly and deliberately out of the restaurant. *It'll only make things worse.*

But once she was out of the stifling restaurant and in the open air, Elizabeth couldn't hold back anymore. And as she felt hot tears mingling with raindrops on her cheeks, she picked up her pace, moving down the parking lot and along a small road, not knowing where she was heading, just knowing she had to move away, had to go somewhere quiet where she could be by herself.

As she sank down beside a parched tree, Elizabeth looked up at the bruised sky, wide and bleak, and felt totally, utterly alone. Alone like she'd never felt before.

I've lost myself! Elizabeth felt giant tears sliding under her chin, but she just let them fall, not even

174

making a move to wipe them away. What was she doing with her life? What was she doing on this stupid trip, shedding pieces of herself with every mile?

I've lost everything—my pride, my sense of identity, everything! Elizabeth thought as a sob racked her body. Everything was out of control, everything sacred ruined by Sam, everything she valued given up for the sake of keeping the team in the contest. If she left now, Elizabeth knew she could get herself back, gain a new perspective on her life. But she also knew she couldn't leave the team, couldn't be a deserter. The price to pay for staying was overwhelming—but what choice did she have? *It's a vicious trap!* Elizabeth reflected miserably, hanging her head in her hands.

"Elizabeth?"

"Just leave me alone," Elizabeth whispered, not wanting to even look at Sam. It was too late for his lame apologies.

"Liz, please?"

Something in the way Sam's voice cracked made Elizabeth look up, almost involuntarily. And seeing him so red-faced, his eyes shining wildly with alarm, made her feel marginally better about how she must look. Sam appeared to be freaked out in a way Elizabeth had never seen him before—not even the one time after the white-water rafting event when he'd broken down and cried on her shoulder. Gone was his usual self-possession, and in its place was the expression of a scared little boy. *That makes two of us I don't recognize!* Elizabeth thought bitterly. Not that she cared.

"What could you possibly want now?" Elizabeth blurted out. She hadn't meant to speak, but it seemed she had nothing more to lose. What did it matter what she said or did at this point?

"I just want to say—"

"You're sorry, right?" Elizabeth cut in bitterly. "I think I've heard that one before."

"Maybe," Sam admitted in a low voice, crouching. "But this is different."

"How?" Elizabeth shot out, her eyes blazing indignantly.

"Look, Liz, we've had our ups and downs and false stops and starts." Sam ran a hand through his hair, his jaw clenched awkwardly. "But I know things have gone too far this time."

"Really! How far is too far, Sam? You make fun of me all the way from Chicago to Louisville, then you dress me down in front of everyone for wanting to get to Nashville in a hurry. And then you pick on me for not wanting to ride shotgun with you when all I wanted to do was take a nap! Now, which part of that is beyond the pale? Which part is any different from all the other times you've attacked me?"

Sam winced with each word Elizabeth hurled at him and remained silent for a moment. *Good! At least he's not going to protest his innocence.*

"OK, first things first. I didn't mean to make fun of you," Sam began quietly. "The Tom Watts jokes were just that—my ragging on him for his idiotic attempt to get your attention at Wrigley Field. I'm sorry if you think I was trying to insult you, but that wasn't my plan."

"Well, you could have fooled me!" Elizabeth turned away from Sam, shaking her head. It wasn't as if she hadn't seen the teasing coming, but hearing Tom's declaration of love in the form of several tasteless knock-knock jokes delivered by Sam to Josh had seemed in particularly poor style.

"Liz, please. I know I'm not very good at this stuff, but I don't want us to be enemies," Sam continued, nervously twisting the silver Navajo thumb ring he wore on his right hand. "It takes two to tango, you know, and you had been giving me the cold shoulder all morning."

"That's because—," Elizabeth began, but Sam silenced her with a hand.

"What difference does it make?" he said impatiently. "It's always a chicken-or-egg situation with us. The main thing is, I'm sorry. I really didn't mean to upset you like this. But I never thought you'd take my ragging all so seriously. You usually fight back pretty tough, you know. I think you have to remember to take everything I say with a pinch of salt," Sam added with an awkward smile.

"No kidding! A trough of salt is more appropriate," Elizabeth replied. But although she still felt raw, something about what Sam was saying, or maybe something in his tone, softened the defense mechanism inside her. Not for the first time she wondered if she wasn't being hypersensitive and if perhaps she wasn't at fault for allowing Sam to be the barometer for her feelings. *He may be a chameleon, but you don't have to be!* she reminded herself.

"I meant what I said when I asked for a truce the last time," Sam said with a tense smile. "You don't have to like me, but it would be great if you could try."

"Hmmph." Elizabeth sifted her hand through some loose gravel and considered Sam's words. Hadn't they come a bit too far for apologies and fresh beginnings? And if Sam really wanted to be friends, then why were they at this same point for at least the second time in two weeks?

"Tell you what, Liz. I'll make you a solemn promise: No more teasing and no more smart remarks on my part if you promise to stop making me so nervous."

"Huh?" This was out of left field. Elizabeth was intrigued. "Since when do I make *you* nervous?"

"Since always!" Sam laughed. "Like now. I'm totally terrified. Why do you think I always react so badly when you criticize me? I feel like I'm on trial all the time, and it's hard not to mess up when I know you've already written me off as a schmuck."

"Me?" Elizabeth couldn't believe what Sam was saying, but if he was being honest, well, that cast a new light on things. *Mr. Cool, Calm, and Collected—afraid of me?* But as she looked at Sam, on his feet again, his hands thrust deep in his pockets, his eyes averted, she could see he wasn't joking. For once the trickster appeared vulnerable, and Elizabeth could see this was a moment of honesty. A rare moment, but one that couldn't be ignored altogether.

Suddenly Elizabeth didn't feel so squashed by Sam's presence because just as suddenly, he began to look like a regular guy to her—someone with the same flaws and confusions and good points as every other guy she'd ever met.

"I guess I can be a little reactionary. Maybe even too critical sometimes," Elizabeth admitted finally.

"Hey, guys, let's go! It has stopped raining," Uli shouted from outside the Winnebago.

"Peace, then?" Sam asked, offering his hand to help her up.

"I'll think it over," Elizabeth replied with a small, conciliatory smile, accepting Sam's hand.

She wouldn't make Sam any promises of friendship, not just yet. But as she looked up at the sky, Elizabeth noticed a ray of sunshine peeking through the clouds. Maybe things were clearing up after all.

179

Chapter
Fourteen

"Okeydokey, folkies, it's time for the Grand Ole Opry!" Richie Valentine exclaimed in an annoying singsong voice. "And here we are, ladies and gents. You guessed it! It's Amateur Night at the Grand Ole Opry in Nashville, Tennessee, and it's also time for eeeeevent number six! Yes, sirree-bob, our kids are about to find out just what it is they're in for! And they're going to find out right now, and right here where generations of country stars were born, from Dolly Parton to George Strait!" Richie paused dramatically. "Event six—the mystery is about to be revealed."

Like we don't know it already, dweeb! Jessica rolled her eyes and slouched farther into her seat. Clearly Richie was fifty million brain cells short of a brain if he thought tonight's event wasn't self-evident.

"Tonight our young guys and gals are going to

be performing country favorites for points—off-the-cuff, nonrehearsed, and live before your very own eyes. That's right, everyone, our gang's gonna be singing for their supper!" Richie continued. Jessica caught a glimpse of Pam out of the corner of her eye. She was all decked out in a gaudy rhinestone-studded miniskirt.

Smoothing the skirt of her own fabulous gown, Jessica said a silent "thank you" that she was born with a natural sense of fashion. In a stark but shimmery white, Marilyn Monroe–type dress with a plunging V neck and just a few strategically placed rhinestones, Jessica had managed to turn herself out country style, but country style with Jessica Wakefield panache. After all, there was a fine line between over the top and just plain hideous. Of course, the dress had bruised her emergency American Express, but Jessica felt she deserved it. Just having to endure the Nashville event was worth its weight in Platinum Plus—and definitely constituted an emergency.

"All teams must perform at least two numbers, group or solo. The team that embarrasses itself least, according to the crowd gathered here tonight, will win. And the second, third, and fourth places will also be determined by popular vote!"

As the crowd cheered, Richie tipped his gigantic cowboy hat and Jessica cringed. The man was truly repulsive, especially in his pseudocowboy garb. In fact, the only man who'd managed to muster up a palatable country-western outfit was Neil, who, Jessica had to admit, looked pretty gorgeous in his jet-black Western shirt, slim-fitting jeans, and slick, black hat.

Pity we won't be doing a duet, Jessica mused wistfully as Neil huddled with the rest of the team. At this point there was enough ice between the two of them to sink several *Titanic*s, and Jessica wasn't about to melt it.

"Jessica, how about you?" Todd proposed. "You can sing."

"Forget it," Jessica replied coldly. "I'm not in the mood."

"I'll sing!" Pam suggested, her voice shaking with excitement. "I've had tons of singing lessons. It'll be a cinch."

"Really?" Jessica retorted caustically.

"Seriously, Pam is amazing," Rob argued as Neil and Tom exchanged a skeptical look.

"Let's see her in action," Jessica replied smoothly, shooting Pam a broad, fake smile. "I'm all for it."

This ought to be worth the loss in points! Jessica sat back smugly, watching as Pam rushed forward, practically tripping over the onstage microphone. The pleasure of seeing Pam lose face on national television was something for which Jessica would happily forfeit any chance of winning the stupid road-trip competition. Not that losing mattered— she couldn't care less about Coast-to-Coast anyway.

All she wanted was to get home—or go back to Memphis.

Jessica swallowed, a twinge of sadness gripping her as she thought of Elvis. She'd been trying to call him all day, but the answering-service number he'd given her wasn't working. *Maybe I'll never see him again,* she thought miserably. *And all for this!* Jessica looked around her, loathing everything animal, vegetable, mineral, and especially *male* she could see. The scene was simply too awful for words.

"And what are you going to sing for us tonight?" the compere demanded of Pam, all teeth and big hair.

"I'm going to do 'Blue,' just like Leann Rimes!" Pam screeched back in her high-pitched, nasal whine.

This is so tacky! Jessica observed gleefully as the backup music kicked in and Pam looked pensively out at the crowds.

But as Pam opened her mouth, Jessica was so surprised, she felt as if she'd sat on a pincushion. Instead of Pam's customary earsplitting squawk, out came a clear-as-a-bell tone, as pure as any country singer's.

"Yeah!" The crowd applauded as Pam continued.

Jessica's mouth dropped open like a trapdoor as Pam continued soulfully. It was unbelievable. For once Pam's twangy vocals actually sounded in place, especially since the girl could actually carry a tune!

Who knew? Jessica thought irritably, cursing herself for pushing Pam onto the stage. Now here was Pam—ugly but admittedly talented—soaking in the adulation of the crowd like a sponge. The situation was beyond unpleasant, and Jessica pursed her mouth into a thin line.

Spare us! she thought nastily as Pam attempted to curtsy in her tight skirt. *Now I guess I'll have to perform!*

Jessica hadn't planned on lowering herself to sing unless she absolutely had to. Not when she was surrounded by tastelessness at every turn. Plus it had seemed like a good way to get back at the team for what they had put her through since abandoning her in South Dakota. But that was no longer a consideration. Not when her ego was at stake.

I'll show her! Jessica plotted, tossing her hair. She knew she could pull a Shania Twain better than Shania herself, and now it appeared she would have to.

You may be on the stage, Jessica thought, glaring at Pam as she twirled around like a spinning top, *but you haven't upstaged me yet!*

"Give it up for Mickey James of Team Four!" the compere announced enthusiastically as the audience whooped and laughed. "Mickey, you ain't no Billy Ray Cyrus, but I think you broke a few achy-breaky hearts tonight!"

185

Mickey bowed and then hollered loudly, much to the audience's amusement—Neil's especially. Although Mickey couldn't sing a note, he sure knew how to get people going. *But he's not the only one!* Neil thought, his eyes twinkling as he sprinted onto the stage for his turn. At Todd's urging, he wasn't listed as Team One's official second entry. That privilege went to Jessica, whom Todd was certain he could convince to perform. No, Neil was just going to help Todd encourage Jessica to be a team player.

Neil passed Jessica and grinned at her, but she didn't return the smile. Not that Neil was surprised. Even the infectious mood at the Opry hadn't changed the sour expression that now seemed a permanent feature on Jessica's face. But hopefully that would change soon enough. Neil knew it was a long shot, but if there was one thing Jessica responded to, it was humor. *And that's one thing I can do!*

"I'll be doing 'Jolene,' by Dolly Parton," Neil announced, taking the microphone and signaling to the band as the audience's cheers died down. "It's a little variation, actually, which I've remodeled around the character of my friend and teammate, Jessica," he added, indicating an alarmed-looking Jessica with a flourish of his hand.

"Jessie-lene, Jessie-lene, Jessie-lene . . .
I'm begging you, honey,
Please don't ditch the team!"

As Neil crooned, the entire theater swelled with laughter and clapping. *Too bad I can't get some points for this!* Neil thought. Not that it mattered. Pam had pretty much ensured the team's win with her amazing star turn, and once Jessica got onstage . . . No, "Jessie-lene" was all about having fun and showing Jessica how silly her grudges really were. It was time to lighten up after the funereal atmosphere of the last week, and if anyone was into bold, brash humor, it was Jessica Wakefield.

"Well, well, well, you're a *runaway* gal . . . ," Neil sang to hoots of laughter. The audience was really getting into it, getting louder and more boisterous as Neil added plaintive phrases, begging Jessica not to "cut loose" or "hit the road!"

Not bad, if I do say so myself! Neil had to admit that he'd done a pretty smart revamp on a tired old number. And judging by the thunderous applause as he finished the song on his knees, his arms outstretched, beseeching "Jessie-lene," the audience was in unanimous agreement. *Almost . . .*

Ouch! Neil blinked as Jessica's pinched face swam into focus, her eyes glowing with red-hot anger. *Not quite unanimous,* Neil realized, Jessica's vengeful glare telescoping toward him.

Apparently his trick hadn't done the trick at all. *And now you're in for it.* Neil didn't know whether

187

to be terrified or amused, but either way he knew he had to prepare himself. He'd just sung the song, but now he had to face the music!

"And for anyone who claims Neil Young isn't country, well, that's a matter of opinion," Sam muttered into the microphone. "I happen to think this song, especially, has some serious country roots."

Here goes! Sam hoisted Ruby's guitar strap over his shoulder and leaned forward on his stool. He'd requested no band for this number. Just a guitar. "Old Man," by Neil Young, was one of Sam's favorite songs, and he wanted to perform it acoustically, without all the flash of a house band.

Sam began singing gruffly, looking down at the guitar so as not to get too nervous. The hushed crowd was more than a little intimidating, but if he closed his eyes, he could pretend he was by himself, singing a song he loved. Although the lyrics were a bit sappy, the song had somehow always moved him.

As his voice gained strength and confidence, Sam lifted his head and opened his eyes. He found himself staring right at Elizabeth. It was weirdly ironic, sitting there singing a love song only to open his eyes and see her. Suddenly the lyrics had gained a focal point. Sam gave her a slight smile, and she smiled back.

Looking directly at Elizabeth was obviously helping his performance. Sam could tell he was really getting a response from the audience. And he in turn responded by singing passionately, honestly, as if he were all alone in the room except for the one person to whom he was singing. Elizabeth.

As Sam struck the last chord, a moment of silence preceded what could only be called deafening applause.

"Thank you," he mumbled into the microphone, somewhat surprised by the wild reception—and by the fact that he'd gotten so swept away. Sure, he knew he was doing pretty well, but he was no star performer, just a regular guy who could strum a guitar and hold a tune. Still, performing was about more than just music. It was about feeling, and Sam knew he'd definitely poured his heart into expressing the emotions the song made him feel.

Good performance! Sam congratulated himself and nodded to the audience. Of course, that was all it was, he reassured himself as he stepped off the stage. Just a performance.

Or was it? Sam fleetingly caught Elizabeth's eye again. He couldn't deny the fact that while he was sitting up there onstage, the lyrics had seemed real and meaningful—words he could relate to on a personal level.

Whoa, now you're getting too heavy! Sam averted

his eyes from Elizabeth's and moved through the crowd offstage. *It was just an act,* Sam told himself sternly. *Let's not get too carried away.* But his protestations struck a false note. There had been more to the song than mere performance, and Sam couldn't deny it any longer.

Now the question was, could he follow his onstage act in real life?

"Aren't you going to sing now?" Todd queried timidly.

"What? Are you insane?" Jessica snapped as Todd stepped back nervously. "I saw you all snickering during Neil's performance!" Jessica's eyes narrowed into paper-thin slits. "If you think I could possibly still have one ounce of loyalty to this team, you all need brain scans!" Jessica stood up, gave Todd, Tom, and the rest of the team her most monstrous glare, and flounced away from their seats.

No way would she deign to get up onstage now and perform. Not after that disgusting display from Neil. *The nerve!* Jessica almost couldn't believe what she'd seen and heard with her very own eyes and ears. And to think she'd ever considered Neil a friend, someone with a decent sense of humor. *So much for that theory!*

"Jess, come on, it was harmless!"

Jessica wheeled around sharply. Just the sight of Neil, a placating smile on his lips, made her so mad, she thought she might spontaneously combust.

"I only wanted to make you laugh. Please do your song," Neil continued.

"Forget it!" Jessica snapped. Neil could beg until the cowboys came home, but her lips would remain zipped.

Of course, it was a crying shame because Jessica knew she could show them all. There was no doubt she could floor the whole theater with her performance, knock Richie Valentine, Ned Jackson, and the rest of the audience right out of their rhinestone-spangled socks.

"Sorry, I'm not interested," Jessica said tersely.

A look of crushing disappointment crossed Neil's face and Jessica almost caved. Almost.

"But Jess, we'll be DQ'd again!" Neil cried out. "My act technically didn't count since my name wasn't submitted as one of our performers. But your name is on the list as one of Team One's contestants."

Jessica only hesitated a split second. "Well, I guess you should have thought first before you chose me without asking my permission!" Jessica was relishing the desperate looks and urgent, pleading glances on her teammates' faces. *Serves them right!*

"Last chance for a Ms. Wakefield from Team One," the compere intoned, squinting into the audience. "Ms. Jessica Wakefield?"

"Please, Jess. *Please!*" Neil begged, practically wringing his hands.

"Forget it, you guys!" Jessica hissed out loudly. "I don't even know how you can call yourself a team when you go around humiliating your teammates."

"Last chance," Richie boomed from the stage as the compere blinked at Jessica. "Jessica, what'll it be?"

Suddenly, with the eyes of the audience on her, Jessica really felt unsure. Once again it was all in her hands. If she sang, Team One undoubtedly would win. If she refused to sing, Team One would be disqualified.

It took only a second for Jessica to evaluate and reevaluate the situation.

Jessica took a deep breath. "I told you," she repeated, her voice firm and steady, "I am not singing."

Jessica folded her arms and stared coolly at her nervous teammates as Richie announced the official disqualification of Team One. *You see?* she thought with pleasure. *You do need me after all! And it's time you realized it!*

"Oh, c'mon, darlin', since when does my Marilyn refuse her place on the stage?" a voice whispered in her ear.

Jessica practically jumped out of her skin. *Could it be?*

"Elvis?" she shrieked, spinning around. It was!

Gorgeous and well groomed as ever, Elvis looked good enough to eat. He was dressed to the nines in a vintage fifties-style suit with a flashy red tie, his hair gleaming with pomade.

"Oh, Elvis!" Jessica practically fell into his arms. "Why, I can't believe it!" she murmured, slipping unconsciously into her southern-belle voice. "How—what are you doing here?"

"I couldn't forgive myself for not driving you to Chicago," Elvis replied teasingly. "So when I heard you were in my neck of the woods, I thought I'd better show up to apologize."

"Oh, come on!" Jessica had to laugh. After all, Elvis had all but forced her to let him drive her to Chicago from Nashville. But it was Jessica who wanted to go it alone—even though she'd regretted her decision every moment of the long, smelly bus ride and every moment since.

"No, seriously, I came to see you up on that stage, honey," Elvis replied, stroking her hair. "And just as soon as they gave out your destination on TV, I jumped in the Caddy and flew."

"Just as well," Jessica answered. "Because I'm ready to split. Perfect timing, E.!"

"Just hold your horses there, Marilyn." Elvis placed two hands firmly on Jessica's shoulders. "Don't be a spoilsport. I'm not leaving without a song."

"Well, sing it yourself. You're Elvis Presley, aren't you?" Jessica retorted huffily. It was too late for songs. Team One had been disqualified anyway.

"A duet is what I had in mind, actually," Elvis answered, a sexy grin spreading across his face. "How 'bout it, baby? You and me?"

"No—," Jessica began vehemently, but Elvis cut her off, silencing her with a finger to her lips.

"Not so fast with that DQ, Mr. Valentine!" he shouted. "Miss Wakefield will be performing after all," he added loudly. "And she'll be performing with me."

A song is just a song—or is it? Elizabeth could have sworn she'd heard some real emotion in Sam's performance. It was almost as if he'd sung that ballad to her alone.

Maybe she was just fooling herself, but Elizabeth couldn't shake the sense that Sam's act hadn't been all for the benefit of the audience. And although it seemed odd, in a way it also made perfect sense. Some people could only reveal themselves onstage. . . .

"We're doing well!" Ruby whispered. Elizabeth smiled in response and sat back, contented. *Things are definitely looking up!* she thought happily. Her own Wynonna and Naomi Judd duet with Ruby had been none too shabby, and Elizabeth could safely wager it had helped put Team Two squarely in the running for first place.

194

"You said it," Elizabeth replied, squeezing Ruby's arm. "We're doing really well!"

In fact, in every way the evening was turning out to be a good one. The only hitch was Jessica's supposed refusal to perform, but even that only made Elizabeth smile and shake her head.

Watching Jessica creating a spectacle, her flashy Elvis-impersonator friend the perfect accessory, Elizabeth had to chuckle. Jessica could huff and puff all she liked, but she didn't fool Elizabeth. Jessica was exactly where she wanted to be—at the center of attention, creating waves as only she knew how to do and loving every minute.

The whole room was cheering now, urging Jessica to get onto the stage.

"C'mon, Jess!" Elizabeth yelled, clapping loudly. But either way, what did it matter if Jessica performed or not? *She doesn't need the stage.* Elizabeth knew that only too well. *Jessica's life is one big performance!*

"Jessica, Jessica, Jessica!" the audience chanted. Jessica surveyed them with cool detachment. Let them yell! All those shiny-faced extras understandably desperate to see the star get up onstage. Who wouldn't be? Jessica knew she looked like a million dollars, especially with Elvis at her elbow. And it was tempting, very tempting, to give the crowd what it wanted. With an effort Jessica restrained herself from rushing up onstage.

But one thing held her back: She had to punish the team, make them atone for what they had done to her.

"Come on, Jess! Everyone wants you up there!" Elvis coaxed.

"No can do!" Jessica replied decisively. She would not—could not—give in.

"Then I guess I'm on my own," Elvis murmured, racing up onto the stage.

Oh, boy! Jessica blinked as Elvis grabbed the mike and began crooning to her in his husky voice, begging her to perform in an impromptu, Elvis-style song that drove the audience berserk.

Don't move! Jessica commanded herself, but her feet in their jeweled satin pumps were just begging to spring up onstage.

It was all too much—the screaming audience, the pull of Elvis's seductive voice! Jessica was weakening, her resolve melting away. Maybe she should just get up there. Maybe punishment wasn't everything—and maybe she ought to show the team, show *Neil,* that she was tough, that she was unstoppable. That they might be able to beat her, but they'd never be able to break her!

Jessica bit her lip, then ducked her head and slowly walked toward the stage. *Like the parting of the Red Sea,* Jessica observed as the reverent crowd split to let her through, their hysteria urging her on as she ascended to her rightful place at Elvis's side.

This is great! Jessica realized as she drank in the bright stage lights, the massive, cheering audience . . . until she realized she had no idea what they were going to sing. Elvis hadn't even asked her what songs she knew! Jessica turned panicked eyes on her partner.

Elvis winked. "You'll be fine," he whispered.

And as the band kicked in, Jessica relaxed. It was Dolly Parton and Kenny Rogers's "Islands in the Stream," a song that she and Elvis had heard over and over again on Tennessee's Classic Radio station while they'd been on the road.

Jessica took a deep breath. OK, so Dolly Parton wasn't exactly a vamp, but Jessica saw no reason why she couldn't spice up her own rendition of the song.

And it seemed Elvis had the same idea for his Kenny Rogers part. As he began to sing, his voice sensual and raw, he grabbed Jessica's hand and pulled her toward him into a forceful spin.

OK, Wakefield, Jessica coached herself, swooning into Elvis's arms, *time to get steamy!* Jessica opened her mouth and delivered her lyrics in a seductive, breathy tone that was far more Marilyn Monroe than cutesy Dolly Parton.

The crowd went insane, and Jessica felt a heady, thrilling rush of pleasure suffusing her entire body. So maybe she didn't trill like Pam or coo like Dolly, but who cared? *Style over substance!* Jessica thought happily as she oozed her final words into the microphone.

"Thank you, thank you all!" Elvis gave a debonair, million-dollar bow and blew kisses at all the screaming women in the front row. He was a seasoned professional, and it showed. For her part Jessica merely glowed with satisfaction, regarding the sea of faces with a regal, indulgent smile.

"Unfortunately that spectacular performance doesn't count," Richie began as Elvis kissed Jessica's hand and twirled her around to further applause. "I had to confer on this one, but we're all in agreement: Miss Wakefield's mystery partner isn't on her team, so I'm afraid we have to disqualify Team One. . . ."

Who cares? Jessica's gaze fell on her discouraged teammates, huddled in a knot in their seats. They looked even more pathetic from up on the stage, their outfits like rags in comparison with her own and Elvis's. *Just a bunch of serfs!* she thought in amusement, putting to good use the only word she remembered from her medieval-history class. Serfs, the lowest class of society! The description was perfect, and if the truth be told, Jessica was overjoyed her team had lost.

"Sorry we couldn't save your team," Elvis murmured, pulling Jessica toward him as they left the stage and made their way back through the crowds.

"That's quite all right." Jessica smiled, snuggling under Elvis's arm and dismissing her teammates with a shrug. *They can go roast a hog or whatever it is they do in Nashville,* she mused, her hand splayed across Elvis's scrumptious, ripped chest. *I'm far more interested in Memphis!*

"And it seems that by popular decision, we have our winner," Richie Valentine yelled as the audience rippled with excitement. "Team Two it is—thanks to Sam Burgess and the lovely and talented Ruby Travers and Elizabeth Wakefield!"

Ruby glowed with pleasure as she stood up to the sounds of clapping and cheering. This was what she was all about—the lights, the stage, the applause all felt so right to her.

I belong here! Ruby thought as her eyes swept the auditorium. Of course, country wasn't quite her style, but she still felt a part of this world—the world of music and performing, where the show was everything and the air crackled with energy.

"And now for the final rundown. Team Two leads at 180 points—that's thirty points ahead of Team Four, in second place!" Richie's announcement was drowned out by further applause, and Ruby hugged Elizabeth, on a high from their overall win, their success that night, all of it!

"Team Three is in third with 130, which leaves poor old Team One straggling behind at 110, unable to keep up due to their many disqualifications."

Richie droned on, but Ruby barely listened, her head full as she digested the success of the evening. *What a rush!* The thrill of being up on a giant stage, strutting her stuff before hundreds of eager audience members, giving her soul to the music. And in a historic setting, a place where dreams were made. *Maybe mine too!* Ruby thought, her finger absentmindedly tracing a sparkling red stone on the buckle of her belt.

It was possible. Especially with millions of people tuning in to watch the ICSN-sponsored show. It was a fair bet that at least someone watching had to be a record producer. *And maybe he noticed me!* Ruby thought, a thrill of anticipation kicking at her insides.

Or maybe not. As she cast her eyes lovingly across the Grand Ole Opry stage one last time, Ruby suddenly realized it didn't matter whether she'd been spotted on TV or not.

Only the music matters. And Ruby was beginning to see that more and more.

Chapter
Fifteen

"All right! And swing your pardners!" the band leader twanged as the fiddles and guitars went crazy.

"Yikes!" Elizabeth laughed as Uli and Ruby narrowly avoided crashing into her. Who knew that square dancing could be so much fun? Not that they were really square dancing, but everyone was giving it a valiant try.

"See ya!" Danny laughed as he passed Elizabeth on to the next person. *Sam.* Elizabeth's heart jumped, but she only smiled as Sam grabbed her arm.

"Having fun?" Sam yelled as he swung her around. Elizabeth nodded, her face flushed with pleasure. *And I'm not the only one!* she noted happily. Even Sam seemed caught up in the vibey atmosphere of the hoedown after-event party. Or maybe he was just pleased with himself for pulling Team Two through to a victory!

201

"You were really great out there," Elizabeth complimented Sam as he twirled her into a spin. "Thanks to you, we won."

"You weren't so bad yourself," Sam replied, his lips grazing Elizabeth's ear as he pulled her into an expert dip.

Elizabeth shivered, a thrilling tingle swimming through her body. It seemed as if everything was frozen for one, amazing moment—she lay in the crook of Sam's arm, he looked down at her tenderly, his strong jaw bathed in the refracted light of the disco ball—and then she was up again, spinning around, letting the skirt of her simple but sparkly pale blue dress fan out around her bare legs.

"Guess it's on to the next partner," Elizabeth said airily as she spotted Tom heading down the line.

"You come back here," Sam ordered Elizabeth in a teasing tone, pulling her in and clasping his arms firmly around her waist. "I'm not about to hand you down the line."

Elizabeth stared into Sam's eyes and felt as if she were drowning. Sam looked so intense, as if he had a million things to say.

"You look beautiful tonight," Sam said simply after what seemed like forever.

"And you look very uncountry!" Elizabeth laughed, gesturing at Sam's getup—baggy jeans, sneakers, and a navy T-shirt. "So, what's with the no-cowboy-boots policy?" she joked.

"Got an image to protect! I've got to stay cool and removed," he added with a chuckle.

Elizabeth laughed as Sam pulled the spangled scrunchie out of her hair. "You, on the other hand, can let your hair down," he continued, his voice husky. "And with hair like yours, who needs fake glitter?"

Elizabeth flushed as Sam's fingers trailed through her long, loose hair. It was almost too much to believe. *To think only a day ago we were at each other's throats!*

"What do you say we go outside," Sam suggested in a low voice. "Wait, that sounded so sleazy," he added as Elizabeth regarded him warily. "I just wanted to get away from all the noise for a while. So I can really talk to you," he added sheepishly. "There are things I—things I want to say," he finished, his eyes locked onto Elizabeth's.

"OK," Elizabeth murmured, allowing Sam to lead her from the room. But although she walked calmly, her pulse was racing and her stomach felt like a trampoline. Maybe this was it! Maybe Sam was finally ready to confront his fears of commitment and tell her he really cared.

Or maybe he just wants to talk about the stars. Elizabeth knew she might be hoping for too much, but she couldn't help wanting to suspend the cynicism that had always colored her dealings with Sam.

It seemed crazy, getting lost in the moment,

203

but then again, maybe this was a moment that might finally be *worth* getting lost in. Maybe this was the moment she'd been waiting for!

Neil took a swig of his beer for good luck and walked up to Jessica, who was whirling around the dance floor with Elvis.

"May I cut in for a second?" Neil asked Elvis, smiling tentatively at Jessica.

"You may not!" Jessica replied harshly, tossing her hair.

"Aw, c'mon, Jess. Dance with your friend!" Elvis stepped back gallantly, and Neil gingerly replaced him, afraid Jessica might swipe at his throat with one of her well-manicured nails.

"Good job on the singing, Jess," Neil began, touching her shoulder. "You were amazing up there."

"And you were pathetic!" Jessica shot back, her eyes flashing angrily.

And here we go again! Neil thought grimly, but he refused to back down. Jessica could freeze him if that's what she really wanted, but he would apologize, and she would hear him out.

"I *am* really sorry," Neil offered meekly, "but you have to believe me—I wasn't trying to be malicious!"

"Save it!" Jessica retorted savagely. "Because I don't believe it!"

Neil stared at Jessica. She was refusing to budge one inch, both on the dance floor and in every other sense. Suddenly Neil realized it was fruitless trying to communicate with her. And he'd had enough. Enough begging, enough pleading with her to be reasonable, and enough of her angry flounces and acid stares.

"You know what? I *will* save it!" Neil responded viciously. "I'll save my friendship for those who really deserve it!"

"Good!" Jessica was shaking with fury. "Suits me down to the ground!"

"You're so busy lording it over everyone from your high horse," Neil shot back, "I doubt you even know what the ground looks like anymore!"

Disgusted, Neil turned around and walked away, leaving a flabbergasted Jessica behind him. *And that's the way it's gonna stay!* Neil fumed. He was tired of trying, tired of apologizing and getting nothing but self-righteous anger for his troubles. *If she can't let bygones be bygones, then that's fine by me.* One thing was for sure, there would be no more olive branches for Jessica.

It was time to cut her off.

"Want me to do the dip on you?" Uli yelled, his pale, Nordic skin flushed beet red from exertion.

"No thanks," Charlie murmured. Right then, being dipped was the last thing Charlie wanted. The very thought was enough to make her stomach churn—as if it wasn't flip flopping enough already.

But you made it through the event, Charlie consoled herself. *And you'll make it through this dance!*

Charlie pasted a smile on her face and waved as Ruby whirled past her. If she could keep up the act for just another hour, Charlie knew no one would find it funny if she decided to go back to the Winnebago early. She just had to keep suspicion at bay—which was easier said than done when she felt like something had sucked all the energy out of her.

If only Scott were here! Charlie knew she'd feel OK if she was in Scott's arms, but he'd made a detour in Kansas to visit his aunt and wouldn't be joining up again with the team for a few days. *Scott . . .* Charlie needed him now like she'd never needed him before. Because she needed to know for sure what was really happening to her. And she didn't want to find out alone.

"You are all right, yes?" Uli queried suddenly, thrusting his face up close to Charlie's and scrutinizing her with piercing, ice blue eyes.

"Yes, fine," Charlie stammered weakly, trying to keep pace with the music. But the swaying, whirling couples, combined with the blinding flashes of rhinestone-studded belts and shirts, made her stomach seesaw and her head spin faster than the disco ball above.

"She's been sick ever since those Wrigley Field hot dogs," Charlie heard Ruby mumble, and then she saw Josh lurching toward her, but his face was all blurry.

"I'm fine," Charlie slurred, stumbling as she felt someone take her elbow. "I just need some air." But even her own voice sounded far away, and as she took a step forward, the room felt like a sinking ship, teetering and tipping from one side to the other. It was hard to stand up straight.

"Is that true, honey? You've got food poisoning?" Charlie heard an adult's voice. Ned Jackson's? She couldn't tell—the voice sounded all funny and slowed down.

"Not food poisoning," Charlie mumbled. "It's not that."

"Then what's wrong?" another concerned voice broke in, but Charlie couldn't answer.

All she felt was a sickening dizziness as the room spun faster and faster, the lights shining brighter and brighter. *I can't feel my feet!* Charlie thought in horror. And then she was falling.

And then everything started to turn black.

"Catch her! She's fainting!" Ruby yelled, turning away from Josh as Tom and Uli rushed to break Charlie's fall.

"Let's get her outside," Ruby commanded urgently. Tom picked up Charlie, and Ruby pushed forward, making way between the thickly clustered bodies. After what seemed like ages, they finally got through the door and out into the cool air.

"Let's set her down here," Ruby suggested, and Tom gently placed Charlie onto a plastic chair. "Water!"

"Boy, my head is spinning," Charlie murmured, accepting a cup filled with ice water. "Thanks," she mumbled, looking up warily into a sea of concerned faces. "But I'm fine now."

"No, you're not," Ruby replied sternly. "You haven't been fine in days."

"It must be the hot dogs," Uli broke in. "Even I still feel the sickness from them. Ugh!" He clutched his stomach. But Charlie only shook her head and then fell silent.

"If it's not that, what is it?" Ruby coaxed softly. "Come on, Charlie. Tell me."

"Just a little disoriented spell. I get those sometimes," Charlie replied feebly.

"Sometimes! More like every other day!" Ruby exclaimed, but Charlie wouldn't say anything more. "Come on, I'll take you back to the Winnebago. Tom, give us a hand."

"Sure," he said. With Tom's help Ruby helped Charlie stand and led her away.

Charlie was as silent as a stone all the way to the Winnebago. *Maybe she'll tell me in private,* Ruby hoped, even though she knew that was a long shot.

"Tom, get Liz, OK?" Ruby whispered as Charlie excused herself and went to the bathroom. Ruby had a bad feeling about this. And she knew she needed reinforcement if she was going to get

Charlie to open up. Maybe if Charlie was surrounded by close women friends, she would talk.

"I don't know where she is," Tom replied. "I've been looking for her for ages."

"Last I saw her, she was going out back with Sam," Ruby replied, her eyes on the bathroom door.

"With Sam?" Tom sounded surprised and jealous. But Ruby had no time for all that now.

"Just get her!" she demanded impatiently.

Alone, Ruby gently tapped at the bathroom door, but Charlie didn't answer. *Give her another minute,* she told herself. But after at least an agonizing two minutes had gone by, Ruby couldn't wait anymore.

"Charlie?" Nothing. "Charlie?" Ruby called out again, urgently. She pressed her ear to the door and heard a muffled sob.

"I'm coming in." Ruby jiggled the door handle. But it was locked.

"Unlock the door!" Ruby was almost shouting now, her heart clanging against her rib cage in fear. But all she could hear was the sound of Charlie softly crying.

Come quickly, Liz! Ruby prayed. Elizabeth would know what to do. And clearly something had to be done. Ruby hadn't a clue what was going on, but she knew something was up. And whatever it was, it was serious.

"Liz is out back with Sam?" Tom and Todd exchanged a look. Tom had immediately gone to find

Todd in the club after he'd heard the latest about Elizabeth and Sam. It didn't sound good at all.

Not that I should be surprised, Tom thought grimly. He'd seen Sam's moves, the love song he'd sung at the Opry, designed to flatter Elizabeth and make her feel special, and then the way he'd monopolized her on the dance floor. The guy was working it like a pro.

"Sleazebag!" Tom exclaimed angrily. "He just wants to get his hands all over her. He's like a predator, picking his moment to move in for the kill!"

"He's slick," Todd concurred, his jaw tensed in anger. "One moment he ignores her, the next he's singing her some lovey-dovey number to make her feel like she's the chosen one. But it won't last."

"Not for a day!" Tom added. "He'll treat her like dirt tomorrow."

"You got that right!"

Tom drained the rest of his beer. He knew Sam was a crafty weasel, but he also knew Elizabeth Wakefield. He knew she was smart enough not to get too carried away. *Maybe she's flattered, but she won't fall totally for his act,* he told himself. *Or will she?*

She already has! another inner voice prompted, and Tom shivered as he pictured Elizabeth during Sam's country serenade. She'd been practically in a trance, her eyes glazed—and glued to Sam. Was he too late to cut things off between Sam and Elizabeth before they got out of hand? Maybe. But he'd have to act fast.

"I think this is our moment," Tom declared.

"We've got to put a stop to this." He crushed the beer can in his hand. "That jerk needs some serious straightening out, and I'm not going to wait any longer!"

Burgess isn't the only guy Elizabeth notices, Tom told himself. After all, he'd happened to see her clap when he'd sung a pretty right-on Garth Brooks number at the Opry.

Suddenly Tom felt powerful. Of course, he wasn't going to punch Sam out or anything—not unless he had to—but the situation called for a little intimidation, and Tom was more than ready to rise to the occasion. "You in?" he queried as Todd drained the contents of his brew.

"You bet!" Todd agreed. "Let's go!"

The two guys went out the front door of the club. As they rounded the corner of the building, Tom planned all the things he would say when he saw Sam sweet talking Elizabeth. He would politely ask Elizabeth to step aside while the guys had their little talk. And then once Sam had left the scene, he'd gently explain it all to Elizabeth. Tell her he was only looking out for her own good.

"They should be right around this—whoa!" Todd cried.

Tom froze in his tracks, his body as cold and still as marble, his mind barely able to process what was undeniably before his eyes: Elizabeth and Sam—locking lips!

211

Chapter Sixteen

"What the—?" One moment Elizabeth was kissing him, the next moment she'd jumped away from him as if she'd been stung. And then he saw why. Wilkins and Watts, standing there watching them!

"Oh, uh, we were just—," Elizabeth began weakly, stumbling for words.

"We were just trying to have a *private moment!*" Sam finished angrily. "What are you guys—her shadow?" He'd had just about all he could take from Tom and Todd. They'd been watching his every move throughout the evening like they were staking him out for a hit.

"Get lost!" he added, enraged. The dorks hadn't even had the sense to turn around and leave. If anything, they were looking at Sam as if he were the one who had interrupted the romantic scene.

"Just a second, pal," Tom shot back. "Watch your tone!"

"Watch yours!" Sam spat. "You're way out of line here!" Tom took a step forward.

"Hold it!" Elizabeth cried out. "Sam, Tom, calm down. Please!" She laid a hand on Tom's shaking arm. "I'm sorry you, uh, saw this," she fumbled. "I mean, I know you're upset. . . ."

Whose side is she on? Sam's head snapped around, and he glared at Elizabeth. Her flushed face told him all he needed to know. *She's embarrassed to be seen with me!* Sam shook his head. It was all screwed up. Tom and Todd should be embarrassed, and Elizabeth should be angry with them. But instead she was trying to pacify the intruders!

"So, what's this? The ex-boyfriend comes to check up on you?" Sam demanded coldly as Elizabeth murmured something to Tom.

"Make that ex-boy*friends,* plural!" Todd corrected. "Liz means a lot to both of us, and neither of us wants her to get mixed up with a player like you!"

Wilkins too? Sam was stunned. Enraged. Elizabeth hadn't offered a word to argue Todd's proclamation. Instead she was staring at the ground, red-faced. *Unbelievable!* For the past two weeks Sam had thought Elizabeth was the serious type, when in fact she appeared to be running around with half of Sweet Valley University!

"Guys, please! Stop fighting over me. I'm not some object," Elizabeth said finally in a low voice.

214

"Fine by me," Sam mumbled. He turned away, leaving Elizabeth to her two exes. The moment he'd shared with Elizabeth was ruined anyway.

And after what he'd just seen and heard, Sam wasn't sure he really wanted that moment back.

"You still shouldn't have ambushed me like this!" Elizabeth lectured Tom and Todd. "I can't imagine what you were thinking. You guys need to butt out of my life! You totally embarrassed me," she added, her voice shaking. *Not to mention killed a perfectly romantic moment.*

Elizabeth was still angry with Tom and Todd, but she could summon no more strength to reprimand them. She was still mortified to have been caught in a major clinch—and by two exboyfriends! The whole situation would have been excruciating for any woman, and with Sam stalking off . . . Elizabeth didn't know what to think. *Maybe I should have run after him,* she wondered. But then again, she hadn't been very impressed with Sam's childish outburst.

And there was also Tom to deal with. He was the most upset, and Elizabeth couldn't help but feel a pang of sympathy for him. *We didn't break up that long ago,* she realized. *And it wasn't his idea.*

"Look, Tom," Elizabeth began slowly, "I know it wasn't easy for you to see Sam kissing me, but what did you expect?"

"Expect?" Tom's eyes blazed with pain and anger. "I'll tell you what I expected. I thought I could still get through to you, Liz. That's why I came on this stupid trip—to reconnect with you."

"What are you talking about?" Elizabeth snapped. She'd tried to show Tom some sympathy, but now he was getting carried away, and she didn't have the patience for it. Not after all the drama she'd been through in the past two weeks.

"Are you blind?" Tom retorted coldly. "You saw me making a fool of myself at Wrigley. Put two and two together, Liz. Or rather, don't!" he added vehemently. "I guess I was wrong to think we could work things out between us again—especially since you seem to have your heart set on slumming it with the likes of Burgess!"

"Can we talk about this some other time?" Elizabeth spluttered finally. "I'm not going to listen to you tearing Sam to shreds, and as for the rest . . . I can't deal with it right now." *That's an understatement!* Elizabeth thought wryly. If she had to go through yet another public spectacle, she thought she might explode into hives.

"Let's just drop the whole thing," Tom replied sourly. "I've seen enough."

"I'm sorry," Elizabeth finished awkwardly as Tom and Todd turned and walked off. Elizabeth was grateful to see Ruby running over toward her. *Saved!* And not a moment too soon. She'd had enough of Tom and Todd—enough of all the men in her life.

"Liz! Quick!" Ruby panted. "It's Charlie!"

"What? OK!" Elizabeth replied as Ruby motioned at her impatiently.

"I'll fill you in on the way." Ruby hurriedly told Elizabeth the story. "Now she won't come out of the bathroom, and she won't stop crying either," Ruby continued.

I knew something was up, Elizabeth thought. But confirmation of her fears didn't bring any comfort. Charlie's problem was clearly a bad one, and Elizabeth was more than a little afraid.

"We'll get her to talk," Elizabeth consoled Ruby. "And we'll calm her down." As Elizabeth neared the Winnebago and heard Charlie's racking sobs coming through the bathroom window, her body seized up with tension and a terrifying thought crept up on her: Was Charlie dangerously ill? And were they running out of time?

You can't hide forever. . . . Charlie leaned against the cool pane of the bathroom mirror and closed her eyes. Although she knew she had to leave the tiny cubicle sooner or later, she couldn't bear the thought. It was as if by staying in the bathroom, she could shut the world out and make time stand still. But Charlie also knew the game was up. She could no longer hold in her pain, and

217

now that she knew for sure, she had to go out there and deal with it.

"Thank goodness," Ruby whispered as Charlie unlocked the door and stepped out.

"Please, tell us what's wrong," Elizabeth began gently as Charlie brought a Kleenex to her swollen, pink eyes.

Charlie took a ragged breath and sank down onto a fold-out couch, bringing her hands up to her tear-stained cheeks. *Stop crying!* she commanded herself, grinding her fists into the hollows of her eye sockets. She had to be strong now. Now that her worst fears were confirmed, there was nothing else to do but brace herself for whatever would come next and steel herself against dissolving into self-pity.

"You can tell us anything," Ruby whispered gently as Elizabeth put an arm around Charlie's shoulders. "We're here for you."

Anything . . . The word echoed through Charlie's head. Part of her just wanted to get her secret off her chest so she wouldn't feel alone with her pain. But another part of her shied away from speaking, as if speaking itself were the key to making it all real. Silence would keep her safe.

But looking into the concerned faces of her two friends, Charlie knew she had to tell. It was the only way forward.

Just say it! she coached herself as tiny tears sprang into the corners of her eyes. *You have to!*

Charlie opened her mouth and clenched her hands in her lap. Her heart beat like a trapped bird in her chest.

"What is it, Charlie?" Elizabeth prompted quietly.

Charlie spoke in a quiet but audible murmur.

"I'm pregnant."

"Do you really have to go?" Jessica whispered, wrapping her arms around Elvis's neck. "I'd love it if you stayed."

"So would I, darlin', but you know I can't do that," Elvis replied with a sad smile as he threaded his hands through Jessica's hair.

"But can't you trail behind us?" Jessica whimpered. "Pretty please?" she wheedled, lowering her glam-glitter eyelashes seductively.

"You know I'd love to." Elvis groaned. "But duty calls. I got a gig in Memphis tomorrow night."

"OK." Jessica sighed, pouting. Why was it that every time she found herself a great guy, he disappeared faster than pizza in a frat house? *And I'm left with all the losers!* Jessica thought, her face screwing up with distaste as she thought of the trip ahead. It would be one big yawn fest without Elvis.

"Don't fret, Jessie girl," Elvis teased. "We can say good-bye, but good-bye isn't forever, you know. You can always come back to Memphis once the road show's over."

"I guess," Jessica retorted glumly. "But wouldn't it be nice if I could leave right now?" she added emphatically, brightening at the thought. *It's not like I have anything better to do!* Jessica traced Elvis's jawline with the tip of a silver-painted fingernail, a faraway smile on her face. There was no reason to stay, and if experience was anything to go by, every reason in the world to burn some rubber in the trusty old Caddy. "Why waste an opportunity?" she continued in a silky voice.

"Because you have other places to be," Elvis replied, gently loosening his grip on Jessica's waist.

"Huh?" Jessica frowned. This wasn't in the script! Since when would Elvis, of all people, refuse a golden opportunity to spirit her away in his Caddy? *Is he on drugs?* Jessica thought crossly. *I'm ready to follow those blue suede shoes, and he wants me to dig in my pumps and stay here?*

"Oh, baby, you know I'd love to steal you away," Elvis explained in a regretful tone, stroking her cheek. "But that just ain't right!"

"Didn't stop you before!" Jessica wailed plaintively.

"That was different. You needed your space, and you took it. But honey, you can't run away from your troubles forever."

"Of course you can!" Jessica snapped crossly. "And frankly, this lecture is getting a tad tedious.

Let's go," she added impatiently. "Open the door."

"Jess!" Elvis caught her hand and reeled her back into his arms. "C'mon, sweetheart, be real. You know just as well as I do that you have to see this competition through. You won't be happy if you don't," he added.

Jessica bit her lip. Although she hated to admit it, deep down she knew Elvis was right. She couldn't exactly leave her whole life behind, and besides, Memphis didn't even appear to have a decent cappuccino joint. But staying meant dealing with Neil and living in captivity for another two weeks with Pam, Rob, and Elizabeth's megabugging ex-boyfriends. Not exactly a joyride. "You're right," Jessica admitted grudgingly. "But I'll miss you!" She planted her lips on Elvis's neck and inhaled the light but heady masculine cologne he wore.

"You'll be fine, kiddo," Elvis replied softly. "But only if you go easy on those teammates of yours," he added. "Quitting is bad, but bearing grudges is even worse," he continued.

"But they all hate me!" Jessica bleated. "And it's not my fault!"

"Well, then be the bigger person and make up with them!" Elvis suggested. "And besides, no one hates you. I can tell that Neil really cares. . . ."

"Neil!" Jessica blanched. *Yeah, right! He probably thinks I'm Medusa incarnate!*

"Look, Jess, what goes around comes around.

Just do right by your friends—that's all I'm saying."

Friends! What friends? But as Jessica tipped her chin in preparation for a final kiss, she couldn't ignore Elvis's words altogether. Maybe the team deserved what they'd gotten, but maybe she had been a little too harsh on them. Anyway, Jessica didn't want to stay mad forever. For one thing, anger was a toxin—at least, that's what Lila always said. And Jessica could have sworn she felt a zit threatening to break out on her forehead.

Be the bigger person. . . . Elvis's words rang in her ear as his lips crushed her mouth for a last, sweet kiss.

"We'll always have Graceland," he called out a moment later as he hopped into the Caddy.

"Amen!" Jessica drawled, a bittersweet smile on her face as she waved good-bye to him.

You'll see him again, she told herself as she turned to head back to the party. But in the meantime there were other things to deal with—other people.

I'll be the peacemaker! Jessica thought grandly, lifting her chin. But the team would have to do their part too. Peace didn't come out of nowhere, and if they wanted the pleasure of her company, she would expect a formal apology. *And they should all be darn grateful I'm even giving them a second chance!*

*　　*　　*

222

Face it, Watts, it's over. Tom felt like beating his head to a bloody pulp against a brick wall. How could he have been so stupid as to think he could stop Elizabeth from falling into Sam's arms? *You lost your hold on her long ago!* Tom chided himself.

Still, it was hard to believe that after so much time together, so many breakups and makeups, through all the good times and bad, it had come to this. Nothing!

"I'm going back in. You want another beer?" Todd prompted, but Tom merely shook his head in irritation. Couldn't the guy see he was preoccupied? *Of course not! It's Todd!* As sensitive as a box of rocks.

As Tom sat alone outside the club, staring miserably into the sky, he wondered if he'd ever get over Elizabeth. Or would he be forced to regret their breakup for the rest of his life, comparing every other girl to her? Not that she was coming up so favorably right now, defending the likes of Sam and callously refusing to talk to Tom about his feelings for her.

She'll be sorry one day, Tom told himself sadly. For now it was time to move on. Or at least time to reconsider his approach.

Maybe if I back off . . . Tom contemplated this idea. It had seemed to work for Sam. And maybe an about-face would shock Elizabeth into seeing things differently. *Maybe if I stop running after her, she'll come back!*

Or maybe he was simply fooling himself—
again?

Tom sighed, wishing the man in the moon
would give him some answers. Should he keep
hoping or accept that he'd lost Elizabeth forever?

"I don't know what I'm going to do." Charlie
gulped tearfully. "I was afraid to find out for sure.
But I just took the test, and it's positive—like I
knew it would be!"

"Have you told Scott?" Ruby queried as Elizabeth
hugged Charlie.

"Not yet." Charlie sniffed raggedly and ran a
shaking hand through her tear-dampened hair. "I
don't even know how to tell him."

"You'll work it out," Elizabeth murmured, and
Ruby nodded dumbly. She was still in shock from
the news, and watching Charlie so upset was gut-
wrenching.

This is awful! Ruby thought, feeling tears prickling at her own eyes. Ruby hadn't a clue what she
would do in Charlie's position. Life was hard
enough for one person without having a baby to
consider. *And especially at our age!* There were so
many crucial decisions to make, monumental
struggles to get through. How did any young person deal with being a parent?

"What I decide now will affect the rest of my
life," Charlie uttered, choking back a sob as
Elizabeth and Ruby nodded sympathetically, tears

falling freely down each girl's face. "What am I going to do?"

What can we say? Ruby felt so helpless. Neither she nor Elizabeth could give Charlie any real advice. *Especially not me,* Ruby thought. Although her own situation was hardly the same as Charlie's, it was proof enough that life was a huge challenge. And that every choice was crucial.

"Please, guys, tell me what to do!" Charlie implored.

"We can't do that," Elizabeth replied gently. "But we can tell you that we're here for you, right, Ruby?"

"Liz is right," Ruby murmured. "No one can tell you what path to take. I guess all I can say is: Listen to your heart."

"But I don't know what my heart wants!" Charlie spluttered, her voice rising.

"It'll tell you in time. I really believe that," Ruby soothed. Of course, it was easy to give advice, but Ruby herself knew that sometimes the simplest words were the hardest to live by. Listen to your heart. . . . Stay in school? Or go it alone on the road, with only her guitar and her dreams to live on?

"You'll do the right thing," Ruby said, grabbing Charlie's hand and squeezing it tightly. "And in time you'll know what that is."

And so will you, she thought. Ruby felt she was about to make her own important life decision, and it looked as if all arrows were pointing in favor of her striking out on her own. Another one of her grandmother's sayings suddenly came to mind: *A life lived in regret is no life at all.*

"And so I've made my decision to forgive you all for leaving me stranded—that is, if you ask for my forgiveness," Jessica continued dramatically. "But I think it's time you did," she added, her gaze settling on each member of the team, "because we've had enough squabbling to last us all a lifetime."

"Are you finished?" Tom snapped irritably. "And if not, could you trim down the southern accent? It's getting on my nerves."

Well said! Neil hadn't managed to open his mouth—he was still trying to process what he'd just heard—but he was glad someone had cut Jessica off. He thought if he heard one more patronizing word, he'd tear his hair out. Or Jessica's! *Who does she think she is?* he thought angrily.

The content of Jessica's lecture had been nothing short of galling. Pious comments about the team's "selfish behavior" coupled with grandiose pretensions of forgiveness. *And for what?*

"We didn't leave you behind, Jessica," Neil spluttered at last. "So you can let go of that fantasy, along with the rest of your hallucinations about our motives or behavior. The only one who has anything to apologize for right now is you!"

226

"Darned right!" Pam squeaked in agreement.

"What?" Jessica seethed, her mouth twisting with rage. "Me, apologize? In your dreams, pal!"

"Suit yourself!" Neil shot back. "But I think I speak for all of us when I say that we have had it! We've all been making an effort, and I, for one, have bent over backward for you, but no, that's not enough. What more do you want?"

Neil knew he was getting a little too explosive for his own good, but he didn't care. He'd been bottling up enough anger to exterminate several galaxies, and Jessica had practically begged for it with her precious little speech.

"An apology!" Jessica screeched. "That's what I want! *You* left *me* behind!"

"And maybe it would have been better if you'd *stayed* in South Dakota!" Neil shouted.

"I agree!" Rob chimed in, and the others nodded.

Jessica's eyes widened in surprise and then just as quickly narrowed into razor-thin slits. "Thank you for your honesty," she replied quietly, her words dripping with venom.

Neil was about to backtrack. He hadn't meant to let things get so carried away. But just as he opened his mouth, he thought better of it. *Why save a friendship that isn't worth saving?*

Neil closed his mouth, turned on his heel, and walked away. There was no point in trying to soften the blow this time. *Because I meant what I said!* The days of being Jessica's sacrificial offering were over. Neil would no longer endure any of her abuse.

It's over, he thought with resignation. And although Jessica might not yet know it, this time he really meant it. Because she'd just burned her last bridge.

"Don't cry—it'll be OK." Elizabeth clasped Charlie's hand tightly. She knew her words were hollow. *How can I say it'll be OK? I can't possibly understand what she's going through!*

Elizabeth had suspected something serious was behind Charlie's illness, but she'd never expected pregnancy. Charlie's admission had been like a bolt of lightning coming out of the clear blue sky.

This makes all my problems seem petty and ridiculous, Elizabeth thought soberly. Charlie's crisis was a real wake-up call. Next to that, everything in Elizabeth's life—from Sam to Tom—seemed about as significant as a match falling into a volcano.

"You'll get through this," Elizabeth soothed as Charlie shredded the Kleenex in her hand. "And we'll help you," she added as Ruby hugged Charlie. That was all they could do, just be there for Charlie and help her stay strong. Elizabeth knew that friendship alone wouldn't solve Charlie's problem, but just voicing her support made Elizabeth feel a little less helpless. And hopefully her words would make Charlie realize she wouldn't have to be alone in her darkest hour.

"Hey, girls!" Elizabeth looked up at the sound of Josh's annoyingly cheery voice. *How does he do that?* she thought angrily. Josh had a gift for turning up at all the wrong times. And worse, there was Sam right behind him.

"Can't you see we're busy?" Elizabeth snapped coldly as the guys casually clambered into the Winnebago. "Could we have a little privacy, please?" she added as Charlie struggled to compose herself.

"What, PMS-ing together?" Sam replied with a smirk. "We'd better leave, Josh," he added.

Elizabeth's mouth fell open, and she struggled to find the words to adequately express her anger at Sam's unbelievably sexist statement. "Yes, *leave,*" she hissed, "and take your chauvinism with you!"

"Run, Josh, run," Sam quipped as he turned to go. "We don't want to hang around here," he added pointedly. "Too much grrrl power, wouldn't you say?"

Of all the . . . Elizabeth couldn't even formulate the insulting words in her mind, let alone speak them. "Pigs," she spluttered finally, at which Sam turned around and surveyed her coolly.

"Yes, we are, aren't we?" he added sardonically. "Unlike all those fine, upstanding SVU boyfriends of yours."

Enraged, Elizabeth jumped to her feet, forgetting Charlie, Ruby, and Josh. All she could see was Sam, his face distorted into a mean grin. How could she ever have seen anything valuable in him? He was nothing but a jerk. Tom and Todd were right! The guy was a lowlife, plain and simple.

"Get lost!" Elizabeth retorted in a low, trembling voice. "I mean it," she continued icily, her face a mask of fury. "I want you to get away from me."

And stay away! she added silently. *For good this time.*

Find out what happens as Jessica and Elizabeth ride through the last part of their exciting summer road trip! Don't miss Sweet Valley University #50: **SUMMER OF LOVE.**

You'll always remember your first love.